"Allow me to bring you up to speed," Raffaele murmured, his concentration shot when Maya crossed her legs, revealing for a split second a tiny slice of pale inner thigh that was inexplicably outrageously erotic.

Raffaele clenched his strong jaw, questioning his libido's overreaction to such a tame glimpse of the female body. He didn't like how she turned him on hard and fast. Such reactions didn't come naturally to him—at least they never had before with any other woman.

"You were saying," she prompted, irritating him more.

He gave her a potted history of their families' marital misses and the news about her ancestor's will and the company. Her eyes widened. "But that was really stupid of him... I mean, what if—"

"Exactly," Raffaele interposed. "And all sorts of complications have arisen since with the company, particularly now that they have a dearth of Parisi talent to run it. It's going downhill and I want to acquire it."

Maya glanced up, still mulling over the tangled tale he had spun. "But you can't acquire it," she said. "Not without marrying and producing a child."

Books by Lynne Graham

Harlequin Presents

The Greek's Blackmailed Mistress
The Italian's Inherited Mistress
Indian Prince's Hidden Son

Conveniently Wed!

The Greek's Surprise Christmas Bride

One Night with Consequences

His Cinderella's One-Night Heir

Billionaires at the Altar

The Greek Claims His Shock Heir
The Italian Demands His Heirs
The Sheikh Crowns His Virgin

Cinderella Brides for Billionaires

Cinderella's Royal Secret

Visit the Author Profile page
at Harlequin.com for more titles.

Lynne Graham

THE ITALIAN IN NEED OF AN HEIR

HARLEQUIN
PRESENTS

HARLEQUIN®
PRESENTS®

Recycling programs
for this product may
not exist in your area.

ISBN-13: 978-1-335-89380-2

The Italian in Need of an Heir

Copyright © 2020 by Lynne Graham

This edition published by arrangement with Harlequin Books S.A.

For questions and comments about the quality of this book,
please contact us at CustomerService@Harlequin.com.

Harlequin Enterprises ULC
22 Adelaide St. West, 40th Floor
Toronto, Ontario M5H 4E3, Canada
www.Harlequin.com

Printed in U.S.A.

THE ITALIAN IN NEED OF AN HEIR

CHAPTER ONE

SILHOUETTED AGAINST THE moonlit sky, the huge house outside Naples looked as if it belonged in a gothic horror movie. All it lacked was the ubiquitous thunderstorm to set the scene as it already had bats flying around the turrets, Raffaele Manzini conceded with wry amusement as he climbed out of his car and his bodyguards clambered out of the car behind him.

'Some place,' Sal, the middle-aged head of Raffaele's protection team, remarked, with the privilege of a man who had been responsible for Raffaele's physical safety since he was a child. 'I'm going to stick to you like glue tonight whether you like it or not. I don't trust your great-grandfather. Back in the day, the word is he was a ruthless killer.'

'Probably all smoke and mirrors.' Raffaele laughed.

'He treated your father badly. A man who casts his own grandson out of the family isn't doing right by his own blood and I'd believe him capable of anything.'

Raffaele said nothing, knowing the older man well enough to know that he had always been a fervent believer in the strength and importance of family ties. But the concept of family was meaningless to Raffaele. His mother had suffered brain damage in an adolescent accident and in spite of her unpredictable rages, obsessional behaviour and wild impulses she had still been allowed to raise him, her only child. Not that she, a Spanish billionairess, had done any of the actual raising. Naturally not. Raffaele had been brought up by nannies, few of whom had endured his volatile mother's employment for long. He had never known a hug, physical affection being something his mother had put on the 'grounds for dismissal' list. He had never known his father until he grew into a man. And he had nothing in common with him either.

To be fair, Raffaele had long known that he wasn't quite normal. There was a giant black hole in him where other people had emotion. Very little touched him. Only business, profit and power revved his engines. And just as he knew that, he knew that all that had brought him to his great-grandfather's doorstep was curiosity.

Aldo Manzini might be ninety-one, but he had retained his sinister reputation. Rumours of Mafia connections, corruption and killings, not to mention brutal business tactics, still clung to his name. Even though his son had died, Aldo had still cut his grandson, Tommaso, out of his life for defying him and he had never forgiven him, which made it all the stranger that he should have extended an invitation for Tommaso's son, Raffaele, to visit him at his fortified estate.

And if Raffaele hadn't been bored, he wouldn't have come. It was that simple. Family ties had nothing whatsoever to do with Raffaele's arrival. His heiress mother's death from an epileptic seizure had left him wealthy beyond avarice at eighteen and his own business achievements since then had made him untouchable. On the international stage, he was an infinitely more powerful man than Aldo Manzini had ever been in his Italian home. He was feared, flattered and feted wherever he went. Needless to say, that got tedious.

Boredom set Raffaele's teeth on edge. He had tried to combat it every way he knew how. The turnover of women in his bed had moved even faster. He had skydived, scaled mountains, deep sea–dived, always searching to find what he needed to stop being bored. Because he *knew* how lucky he was to be born healthy and rich and to have the power to get just about anything he wanted. And at the age of twenty-eight, he had had it *all*: the beautiful women, the decadent parties, the travel, the ultimate of life's experiences. And yet, he was *still* bored…

An ancient manservant ushered them into the creepy mansion. The giant hall rejoiced in the antiquated splendour of a bygone age, the very antithesis of what Raffaele liked but, for the first time in a very long time, Raffaele was not bored. A long wood-panelled corridor ornamented with a line of grim family portraits led into what the old man called the 'master's office'. Raffaele was surprised to register that he would have liked a moment or two to study his paternal ancestors but he suppressed that startling impulse, every skin cell in his very tall and powerful body firing as he saw the even older man seated behind the desk with an assistant hovering by his side. He had drawn hawkish features, but his dark eyes were still as keen as a raptor's.

'You're very tall for a Manzini,' Aldo remarked in Italian.

'Must have caught the tall gene,' Raffaele responded in the same language, which he spoke as fluently as he spoke half a dozen other languages.

'Your mother was taller than your father. Couldn't have abided that in a woman,' Aldo admitted.

Raffaele shifted a broad shoulder clad in a casual cotton shirt. 'Presumably you didn't invite me here to get sentimental about my antecedents.'

'Your hair's too long as well,' Aldo commented, unconcerned. 'And you *should* have dressed for the occasion. Dismiss your bodyguard and I will dismiss mine. What I have to tell you is confidential.'

Raffaele angled his head at Sal, who frowned but backed out of the door again obediently, closely followed by Aldo's companion.

'Better,' Aldo pronounced. 'You can pour us a drink if you like.' A gnarled hand indicated the drinks cabinet by the wall. 'A brandy for me.'

Mouth quirking at the old man's strength of character and imperious attitude, which defied the frail shell of a body trapped in a wheelchair, Raffaele crossed the room and it was one of those very rare occasions when he did as someone else told.

'Do you see much of your father?' Aldo enquired as his great-grandson set a brandy goblet down within his reach.

'No. By the time I had access to him, I was an adult. I see him a couple of times a year,' Raffaele responded carelessly.

'Tommaso's a disgrace to the Manzini family, as spineless as a jellyfish!' Aldo proclaimed bitterly.

'He's happy,' Raffaele replied with complete assurance. 'And that, his small business and his family are all he wants out of life. We all have different dreams.'

'I would hazard a guess that a white picket fence and a bunch of kids isn't *your* dream,' the old man murmured very drily.

'It's not, but I don't begrudge my father his,' Raffaele countered, his dark eyes a brilliant gold that flared in warning as he studied his great-grandfather, wanting the miserable old codger to get the message that while he might not be exactly close to his father, Tommaso, his father's second wife or his three little half-sisters, he would protect both him and them from anyone who sought to harm them.

'Let me bring you up to date on old history.' Aldo leant back in his wheelchair.

A whiskey cradled in an elegant brown hand, Raffaele sprawled down in an armchair, hoping it wasn't going to be a long story because he was already beginning to regret the impulse that had brought him.

'When I was twenty-one I was engaged to Giulia Parisi. Our family businesses were competitors. Both our fathers wanted the marriage to take place but, make no mistake—' Aldo lifted his bony chin to punctuate the point '—I was very much in love with her. The week before the wedding I discovered that she was sleeping with one of her cousins and was not the decent young woman I believed. I was young, *hurt*… I jilted her at the altar because I wanted to shame her the way she had shamed me.'

'And?' Raffaele pressed when the old man seemed to be drifting back into the past.

'Her father was enraged by my disrespect and he changed his will. The Parisi business could never be bought or otherwise acquired by a Manzini. It could only pass through a marriage between the two families and the birth of a child.'

Raffaele rolled his eyes. 'A bit short-sighted to say the least—'

'That business is now one of the biggest technology companies in the world,' Aldo informed him, having reached his punchline. 'And if you do what I want you to do it will be *yours*—'

'Which company?' Raffaele prompted, his interest finally engaged as he ran through various names before Aldo nodded confirmation. '*Seriously?* And it could be mine? For the price of a wife and a kid?' His lean bronzed features snapped taut with distaste. 'As you guessed, not my style.'

'Ever since Giulia, it has been my ambition to acquire that company. The question didn't arise with my son's generation because the Parisi clan had no daughters to target but by the time my grandson, Tommaso, was of age, there was a daughter called Lucia available.'

'And my father blew his opportunity,' Raffaele filled in. 'He's already told me that part of the story. You wanted him to marry Lucia but he was already in love with my mother and picked her instead.'

'Great foresight there,' Aldo quipped with

a curled lip. 'She only stayed married to him long enough to have you and then dumped him. How many stepfathers did you have?'

Raffaele shrugged. 'Half a dozen. My father may not have been the sharpest tool in the box, but he was the best of a bad bunch.'

'You don't know the whole story,' Aldo condemned. 'Not only did Tommaso not marry Lucia, but he also *paid* for Lucia and her lover to run off to the UK and escape the wrath of her family using *my* money!'

Raffaele compressed his wide sensual mouth, almost betrayed into laughter by that dire announcement, which still, even after all the years that had passed, seemed to rankle the most with the old man. 'That was enterprising of him,' he pronounced stiffly. 'However, I believe she was already pregnant by her lover and you can hardly have expected my father to still marry her in—'

'Why not?' the old man shrilled at him with lancing bitterness. '*Any* child would have met the terms of the will if he'd married Lucia Parisi!'

Raffaele registered that he was not dealing with a reasonable man and was not at all surprised that his father had fled to the UK and a humble lifestyle far removed from his wealthy beginnings. A quiet, gentle man, Tommaso could never have stood up to the force of his domineering grandfather's personality or his demands. In much the same way, Raffaele's mother, Julieta, had run over Tommaso like a steamroller. 'That was unfortunate,' he said, setting his glass down, resolving to get himself back out of the mansion again without further time wastage.

'But not half as unfortunate as it would be if you were equally blind to the possibilities of marrying a Parisi.'

'I'm not prepared to marry anyone,' Raffaele spelt out with cool finality.

'This one's a beauty though, and you wouldn't have to *stay* married to her,' Aldo Manzini pointed out, tossing a file across the desk. 'Have a look…'

Raffaele had no intention of having a look at some scion of the Parisi clan. The old man was unbalanced and obsessional and Raffaele had had quite sufficient experience of such personalities growing up with his tragically damaged mother. 'I'm not interested. I need neither the money nor the company,' he responded smoothly, rising from his chair.

'Agree to consider it and I will sign over *my* business empire to you here and now. My lawyer is waiting in the next room,' Aldo told him. 'As for the former Lucia Parisi and her family, I already own them lock, stock and barrel.'

'What are you talking about?'

'Lucia married a fool. They're in debt to their eyeballs and I *own* their debts. What do you think I intend to do with them?'

'I couldn't care less,' Raffaele countered truthfully while thinking about that offer of Aldo's business empire. A fading technology company in need of a fresh innovative makeover, the sort of business challenge he most enjoyed. That attracted him, not the money, no, it was the sheer challenge of rebuilding, redesigning, reenergising that kicked his shrewd brain into activity for the first time since he had entered the room. He *enjoyed* order, structure, after the chaotic nature of his childhood.

'And if you want to acquire the other company, which will dovetail perfectly with mine, you marry the beauty. I know that nothing less than a beauty would tempt a man of your…shall we say…appetites?' Aldo savoured, delighted by the reality that he had contrived to freeze Raffaele in his tracks and that the homework he had done on the nature of his great-grandson had paid off.

Like Aldo, Raffaele was a ruthless bastard in business, a tough and demanding employer and bone-deep ambitious. As Aldo had once been, he was a connoisseur of beautiful women. Like Aldo, what excited Raffaele the most was a challenge in the business field. But Raffaele had had too much too soon and too young, too much money, too much success, too many women. He needed something or someone to ground him back in the real world. Inwardly chuckling, Aldo watched Raffaele lifting the file he had, moments earlier, refused to even look at: *the honey trap.*

Raffaele stared down at the colour photograph. She was tall and she was naturally fair with long silky hair to her waist, flawless porcelain skin and eyes the fresh colour of spring ferns. Her features were...perfect, classical. But beautiful women were two a penny in his world and he would sooner have cut off his right arm than marry anyone and have a child. He flipped past the photo and discovered that she had an IQ higher than his own and Raffaele was twice as clever as most people. Now the thought of an intelligent beauty had considerable appeal to a man long convinced that all truly beautiful women were either mad as hatters like his late mother or insipid and shallow and so in love with their own looks that they had never bothered to work on having anything else to offer the world. Maya Campbell, Lucia Parisi's daughter, however, would be another experience entirely…

'I'm handing her to you on a plate. My representatives are already calling in the debts her family owes. You can ride in like a white knight and offer her a rescue package.'

'To be blunt, I'm not the "white knight" type,' Raffaele interposed drily. 'If I go for this, I'll be straight all the way. I don't put on an act. I refuse to be anyone other than who I am.'

'So speaks an immensely privileged young man,' Aldo commented.

A carelessly graceful shrug was Raffaele's response. He had few illusions about his own character but there were few people alive who knew what he had suffered as a child and adolescent, a live toy for a woman with mental health issues to play with, abused one day, over-indulged the next. He didn't do self-pity any more than he did compassion. He didn't trust people and it hadn't harmed him. He didn't *care* about people and it had kept him safe as an adult from the nightmares that had haunted his childhood. If you had no expectations, you didn't get disappointed. That approach worked efficiently for him.

He hoped it would work for Maya Campbell as well because he wanted those companies. He would take them and, whatever it took, he would whip them into shape again, restoring both business enterprises to fresh growth and profitability.

'I'm getting tired,' Aldo was forced to admit, his head starting to droop. 'Will I call in my lawyer?'

Raffaele smiled his very rare smile. 'Thank you for an entertaining experience, Aldo. And the prospect of even more entertainment on the horizon.'

'She *is* a beauty.'

'Not the woman, the businesses!' his great-grandson contradicted in impatient rebuttal.

The papers for the handover of Aldo's estate were already prepared for signature. The lawyer appeared, accompanied by two witnesses, both of whom were doctors.

Only on exiting the mansion did Raffaele learn what had driven Aldo Manzini to his decision to sign over his empire *before* he passed away.

'Dementia,' one of the doctors told him with a shake of his head. 'In a few months, who knows what he will still be capable of doing? At his age, the degeneration can be rapid, and he knows that.'

And an utterly unexpected pang of regret stung Raffaele and he knew he would visit again, whether he married to acquire the second company or not.

'Oh, my word, I've never seen a more beautiful man!' Nicola, the bride-to-be, carolled at Maya's side.

'Where?' One of Maya's other companions demanded to know.

'Over by the bar…isn't he just dreamy?' Nicola sighed in a languishing tone.

Maya flicked an instinctive glance over to the bar and saw *him*. Man whore, her brain labelled instantly. There he was, at least six feet four inches tall, powerfully built but somehow lean and lithe at the same time, lounging back against the bar of the VIP section of the club with a glittering confidence that blazed like an angel's halo. A man supremely comfortable with being the cynosure of every female eye in the room, coolly accustomed to attention and appreciation in spite of the fact that he was dressed down in ripped jeans, a black tee shirt and what looked like motorcycle boots. It was a certainty that he got admired every place he went.

And it showed. He *knew* exactly how gorgeous he was.

Luxuriant black hair brushed his shoulders, a dark shadow of stubble accentuating his strong jaw line and perfect mouth, throwing his swoon-worthy high cheekbones into prominence. Without the stubble, the muscular development and the tousled hair, he might have looked too pretty or clean-cut as some male supermodels did. Nice wallpaper, she categorised him, but very probably highly promiscuous and definitely not her type. That fast, she dismissed him from her interest and glanced away.

But then she didn't 'do' men in the same way as her university friends did. Maya didn't have time to date, and sleeping around for the sake of a quick physical thrill had never appealed to her either. Life was too short to waste on a man. Her soft mouth curled at the thought and she wondered if her utterly hopeless nice guy of a father had ruined her for all other men and embittered her to a certain extent.

After all, her father was a lovely man, loving, good-natured and caring, but when he went into business, he was a disaster and that truth, matched with the debts he had accrued, had dominated Maya's life for far longer than she cared to recall. Her teenaged years had been a blur of bailiffs, debt collectors and threatening letters and the constant worry of how to keep her family fed and safe. She had her parents, her twin sister, Izzy, and Matt, her eleven-year-old brother in a wheelchair, to look after. Izzy never seemed to resent the harsher realities of their lives and the part their feckless parents had played in depriving their daughters of a normal youth. But Maya had often wondered what it would be like to have ordinary self-sufficient parents, who did the caring, rather than relying on their kids to look after them.

And then, just as quickly, she felt like a bad person for even thinking that way, for being mean and selfish and resentful.

It wasn't her parents' fault that they had always been poor. Neither of them had the desirable talents or educational achievements required by employers and, in any case, her

mother had only ever been able to work part-
time hours with a disabled son to look after.
Indeed, Maya had never contrived to work
out how any of her father's car-crash businesses could ever have done well enough to
enable her parents to buy a house in London,
but they had had the house before she and
Izzy were born and that small property was
the only stable element in their catastrophic
financial world. It was the one plus they had
as a family.

Maya had completed two doctorates in
mathematics at university after first gradu-
ating at eighteen. Being a prodigy from an
early age had only two benefits that she recognised. Firstly, academic brilliance had en-
abled her to finance her studies by allowing
her to win scholarships and prizes and, sec-
ondly, it had given her higher earning powers
in part-time jobs and projects that required
a maths whizz. Extra work had always been
available to Maya but had she had a choice
she would have gone into academic research
because, aside of her family's needs, money
didn't mean that much to her. There were so
many more important, lasting things than
cash, she thought ruefully on the dance floor,
wondering why Nicole was giving her mean-

ingful glances until a hand lightly touched her shoulder to attract her attention.

Maya spun round and, even in her very high heels which took her to five feet eleven, she had the unfamiliar experience of having to tip her head back to see the man who had approached her. And it was *him*, the guy from the bar, and she was stunned because she was not a good bet and she would have assumed such a man would have already worked that out for himself. Her outfit was conservative, her demeanour quiet and she didn't drink, all of which should have loudly signalled her unavailability in the 'fun for a night' stakes.

'Join me for a drink,' he told her. He definitely didn't *ask*; it was a command.

Maya simply laughed, plucking an explanatory hand at the silly pink sash she had been forced to wear. 'Sorry, I'm on a girls' night. No men allowed.'

He had dark deep-set eyes as hard as black granite with little gold highlights and he couldn't hide the fact that the rejection had disconcerted him because for a split second those eyes flared like fireworks against a night sky. And she forgave him because close up he was even more devastatingly gorgeous than he had looked at a distance and she assumed that he had little experience of meeting with female dismissal. He emanated an aura of golden vibrancy comprised of bronzed skin, vital good health and leashed masculine energy. And like all men, he had an ego and she had briefly dented it.

'Are you crazy?' Nicole hissed in her ear, grabbing her arm to march her back to their table and tell the rest of the hens what Maya had done.

And there was a whole chorus of voluble protests. The mood did not go in the direction Maya expected. Indeed, her companions were ready to gift-wrap her for him and hand her over. A bunch of arguments in that line came her way unasked for: she was single, allowed to stray from the hen party, should grab male opportunity when it beckoned and was far too much of a nerd to appreciate that a man like that only came along once in a lifetime.

'He said, "Join me for a drink." It wasn't a request, it was an *order*,' Maya told them defensively when she could finally get a word in. 'He's an arrogant bastard.'

'Got to expect some flaws in all that perfection,' someone gibed, unimpressed.

'Are you seriously telling me that a guy like that isn't worth more than sitting in swotting prissily every night over your computer like you do?' someone else piped up.

And Maya's polite smile froze a little because there was envy in those comments and she was, sadly, used to dealing with that, after being horribly bullied at school for her scholastic attainments. Her peers preferred to believe that she had to swot from dawn to dusk to gain the results she did, and she let them believe that even if it was a lie. Evidently a nerdy swot was more acceptable than someone gifted at birth with a photographic memory and an IQ that ran into the highest possible triple figures. Maya had been doing algebra at the age of three; she didn't need to swot.

Raffaele returned to the bar, seriously unsettled. He had wanted to meet her on level ground on his own terms but from the first glimpse she had not met his expectations. She dressed badly: there was no avoiding that obvious flaw. The high-necked black dress she wore had as much shape as a sack but still couldn't hide the length of her show-stopping long legs or the delicacy of her curves at breast and hip. As for her face, she was, unbelievably to Raffaele, a cosmetics-free zone. Her face was *bare*, not even liner or mascara applied. Lucky for her that her porcelain-pale skin was smooth and faultless, he mused irritably, and her green eyes so arresting that she could get away without artificial definition. But she had turned *him* away. Ordering up a rare second drink, Raffaele gritted his perfect white teeth.

Women didn't walk away from Raffaele Manzini. It didn't happen. He was as bemused as if a tame dog had suddenly bitten the hand off him. Other guys got blown off by women, Raffaele *didn't*. She had barely glanced at him, dismissing him instantly, he reasoned, his jaw line clenching even harder. He ordered her a fancy cocktail and sent it over to the table. She waved a bottle of sparkling water in an apologetic gesture in his direction and passed the cocktail over to another woman at the table. By that point Raffaele was ready to strangle her because she wasn't the pushover he had assumed she would be. It annoyed him when those around him refused to fit the frame he had set them in. He departed from the club in a brooding mood, raging frustration bubbling only an inch beneath it as he stole a last lingering glance at her.

Madre di Cristo... For some peculiar reason she looked even more beautiful now, light blonde hair shimmering in a veil down her back as she shimmied her curvy little bottom to the music beat with one of the other women, long perfect legs flashing, that determined little chin at an upward angle, signalling that she didn't give a damn about anything, anyone. Well, she would learn different, Raffaele swore to himself soothingly, denying the all too ready pulse at his groin that had a mind of its own; she would learn *not* to tangle with Raffaele Manzini and expect to walk away free and undamaged.

'I think she's a nice girl…didn't mean any harm.' Sal broke into speech unexpectedly on the pavement as the limo door was flipped open for Raffaele's entry. 'Not your usual hook-up. Nothing flirtatious about her, nothing suggestive in her dress, just not your usual type.'

Raffaele bit out a curse in Italian, enraged by that comforting assurance from a man who was probably closer to a father than any he had ever known.

'I wouldn't know what to do with a nice girl.'

'Most of us marry the nice ones,' Sal riposted cheerfully.

Of course, Sal knew she was a Parisi from the investigation agency he had employed to track her down for Raffaele to meet. And yet they hadn't officially met as yet. Maya Parisi… Raffaele savoured the name. It suited her better than Campbell, which was too ordinary for a blonde that could catch his eye garbed in a dress like a sack and without make-up or silicone or Botox or, indeed, any of the artificial enhancements that Raffaele was more accustomed to finding featured in the women he bedded.

But if he married Maya, it wouldn't be to *keep* her as Sal implied. It would be to bed her and get her pregnant, Raffaele reflected coldly, and strangely enough that idea no longer repulsed him in the way it had only a week earlier. In fact, he discovered it was more of a turn-on for his jaded libido because it was something new, something different. *But* only for a short time until the task was accomplished. And no, he wouldn't be keeping her, he would be corrupting her with pleasure and then discarding her again, which was pretty much the norm for him. After all, the window of his attention span for a woman was notoriously short.

CHAPTER TWO

MAYA WAS TREMBLING and struggling to hide it as she watched her little brother being boarded on the bus that took him to his special school every morning. Matt was grinning as a friend with a similar disability shouted something out to him, an eleven-year-old boy, still wonderfully innocent about the world he and his parents lived in. A world of debt and disaster, she acknowledged wretchedly, as if Matt hadn't already endured enough in life after losing the use of his legs at the age of four following a fall from the ladder of a playground slide.

The bus pulled away and she closed the front door again. In her mind's eye, every word of the letter that had been delivered and the papers that had been served first thing that morning were still etched inside her pounding head. Official documents containing a court summons and a *threatening* letter had disclosed alarming facts she had not known about her family's financial history.

And that her parents should have left her in ignorance was unacceptable. *That* shouldn't have been possible when she had spent years borrowing from one loan company to pay another, performing mathematical acrobatics to stave off her parents' bankruptcy and the loss of the home her little brother needed for security! Her twin, Izzy, had made so many sacrifices too, working in low-paid jobs to earn every extra penny she could and bring it home. Maya was so angry she wanted to scream. A legal summons to court had been served on her parents, threatening them with bankruptcy.

'Don't look at us like that!' Her mother, Lucia gasped, an attractive brunette in her forties, her brown eyes crumpling as she broke down into sobs. 'We c-couldn't *face* telling you the truth!'

'All these years you've allowed me to believe that you *owned* this house and, because I believed you, now *I* could be in trouble for fraudulently helping you to borrow money against an asset that doesn't belong to you!' Maya condemned, out of all patience with her parents, watching stony-faced as her father closed a supportive arm round his sobbing wife's shoulders.

'Maya...*please*,' her father, Rory, begged with tears shining in his own eyes.

Scolding her parents was like kicking newborn puppies. And not for the first time, as she turned away in a mixture of guilt and angry discomfiture she wondered if she was a changeling, because she had nothing whatsoever in common with either her mother or her father. She loved them but she couldn't comprehend the way their minds worked or the dreadful decisions they made, or the half-lies they would employ to evade any nasty truth. But she had, naturally, worked out certain things. Neither of them was particularly bright, neither of them capable of planning or saving or budgeting, so where *had* her sharp calculating brain come from? One of those gene anomalies, she thought with an inner sigh, knowing such rambling reflections were getting her precisely nowhere in the midst of a crisis.

It was also, by far, the worst crisis they had ever faced as a family and she felt sick and shaky and scared, knowing that no matter what she did she could not possibly drag them out of trouble this time around. There was far too much money owed and, even worse, they had not made a single payment on the private loan that had purchased the house they now stood in.

'Not one single repayment in over twenty years,' Maya reminded her parents out loud. 'That means, you don't *own* this house, the person who gave you this loan *owns* this house and now they want the money back or you have to move out.'

'Tommaso wouldn't do that to me,' Lucia protested. 'His family's too rich and he's too kind.'

Maya slapped the letter that had arrived in the post down on the table. 'They're demanding that the loan be repaid immediately and *in full* or they will take the house and sell it. Whoever Tommaso is, he is no longer prepared to wait for his money.'

'Tommaso is a Manzini,' Lucia informed her in an awed tone, as if that surname alone belonged to some godlike clan. 'The man I was supposed to marry, but he didn't want to marry me either. He helped your dad and I to leave Italy and buy a home here.'

'He gave you a loan,' Maya contradicted. 'The money *wasn't* a gift.'

'Well, *we* certainly thought it was a gift,' her father, Rory, confided in a long-suffering tone.

'It doesn't matter what you thought because you were wrong. You signed a loan agreement.'

'But that was only a sham to cover the paperwork for his grandfather's benefit!' her mother piped up. 'Tommaso promised that he would never ask for any of it back.'

'He *lied*.' Maya slapped the letter again and pushed it across for her mother to see the Manzini Finance logo at the top. 'Although I've got to give the guy his due. He did wait for over twenty years to raise the subject and, if we could afford it, I would take this to court to see how it played out because I'm pretty sure it's *not* legal to wait this long to demand a repayment. *But* we don't have a penny to bless ourselves with, so we won't be going to court on that score.'

'Never mind, we've got an appointment with Manzini Finance,' Lucia objected with a sudden insanely inappropriate smile, as if she were pulling a rabbit out of the hat that would magically save them all. 'We'll just explain and it will all be fixed. This is just a misunderstanding, that's all. You're such a worrier. You're getting all worked up over nothing, Maya.'

'You've been summoned to a bankruptcy court as well,' Maya delivered with clarity. 'Nothing is going to protect you from that. Your debts have caught up with you and we don't have the money to repay them. I hate to say it because I'm not a quitter, but this is the end of the road as far as the debts go. Whoever had the bankruptcy summons served probably assumes they can sell the house to cover the debts.'

'If it wasn't for Matt, we could,' her mother burbled as if the earlier conversation had not taken place.

'No, you couldn't, Mum, because you don't own the house,' Maya parried wearily. 'And I'll be keeping the appointment with Manzini Finance, not you and Dad.'

Rory squeezed his wife's shoulder comfortingly. 'Maya understands all this financial stuff better than us,' he said with confident pride in his daughter's abilities. 'She'll sort this out in a trice.'

Maya studied her parents with quivering lips, which she had to compress to stay in control of her tongue. There would be no sorting it out this time. It was a case of pay up and move out, but she supposed only the actual experience of being homeless would persuade her parents that their mindset of running away from their debts was no longer sustainable. And that was all very well, but what about Matt?

It was her kid brother that her heart bled for the most. The house had been specially adapted for his needs and he had a place in a special school nearby. It was unlikely that her family would be able to stay in the same area. He would lose his schooling and his little circle of mates, lose his home and the few freedoms he still had. Even for an able-bodied child that would be a tough proposition but for a disabled child, it was absolutely tragic.

'I wouldn't mind seeing Tommaso again,' her mother sighed. 'He was like my big brother. Honestly, he was the nicest, kindest man.'

'I seriously doubt that someone as important in Manzini Finance as this Tommaso must be will be present at the meeting,' Maya pointed out, striving not to add the reminder that a *nice* guy wouldn't have allowed such a letter to be sent to his pseudo little sister. As usual, her mother's expectations were far

removed from the reality of what was likely
to happen.

'You're probably right,' Lucia conceded.
'As a family member, Tommaso must be very
senior now in his grandfather's business.'

'I need to dress for the appointment,' Maya
pointed out, escaping the small lounge to flee
down the corridor of their semi-detached bun-
galow home into the bedroom she had grown
up in with her twin. It still had bunk beds,
there not being the space for any other option.

It was fortunate that she kept her interview suit at her parents' home, although she
doubted if it mattered what she wore in the
circumstances. Short of selling her soul to the
devil, there was no way anyone was going to
extend further understanding to her financially incompetent parents, but it was equally
fortunate that she had had the foresight to
have her father sign a power of attorney in her
name so that she was able to deal with their
money problems on their behalf. At least that
gave her the scope to *try* to find a resolution.

After all, now that her academic studies
were complete, she had already accepted a
high-earning position as a trader with a top
city firm and would be starting work at the
end of the month. She hadn't yet mentioned

that news to her family because she wasn't exactly looking forward to the prospect. It was ironic that she didn't revere money and the ability to earn lots of it when, right now, her family was in desperate need of cash. Was there the smallest chance that she could pledge most of that future salary towards her parents' debt and gain her family a little breathing space to stay on in the house? It was a far-fetched idea and she knew it, but it was the only offer of repayment she had within her power to make. Maybe someone at Manzini Finance would prove to have a heart but she wasn't her mother: she was a pessimist.

It was a simple fact of life that people who handled money took good care of it to make a profit, and people who didn't or couldn't pay up, like her parents, were a losing investment.

Maya donned her black interview suit and braided her long hair into a more restrained, adult style, her anxious strained green eyes meeting her in the mirror. *Oh, please, God*, she thought fearfully, thinking of her brother's needs, let me be meeting with a man or a woman with a heart…

It was a very fancy office in the centre of the City of London at a prestigious address. Maya was trying not to be impressed but she *was* impressed, by the elegant receptionist clad in designer clothes, the contemporary architectural design of the building and the buzz of a busy city office space that screamed cutting edge and modern. She sat in the waiting area rigid as a stick of rock, reckoning that there was little chance of meeting with compassion in such a place as Manzini Finance.

All smiles, the receptionist approached her to usher her in for her meeting, her attitude almost fawning, which disconcerted Maya, who was good at reading body language. As the door opened she mustered her courage, her eloquence, her top-flight brain and then all of it fell away in a split second when she stared across the vast office at the very tall, well-built and denim-clad man standing there. And it was unnervingly impossible to hang onto her self-discipline when she saw the same guy she had first seen the night of the hen do at the club with her friends.

'What…what are you doing here?' she muttered in disbelief.

Raffaele was never petty, but he enjoyed the sight of Maya being knocked off her cool, self-contained perch, the widening of the witchy green eyes, the faint pink feathering across her cheeks and the surprised pout of her luscious pink lips. He shifted position, his big powerful frame tensing as the cut of his jeans tightened across the groin. He didn't know what it was about her, certainly not the atrociously ugly suit she sported, but she aroused him. And that was fortunate in the circumstances, wasn't it? he reasoned, but he knew he didn't like that instinctive physical reaction to her. He didn't like anything outside his control, didn't want to be troubled by the suspicion that anything with her could mean anything beyond a business deal.

'I am Raffaele Manzini. It was my father who gave your parents the original loan.'

'Tommaso? My mother said he was a very nice man.'

'He is. Unfortunately for you, however, he is no longer involved in Manzini business. He cut ties with his family around the same time as your mother ran away from hers.'

Maya was trying hard not to stare at him but, really, it was very difficult. In a dark nightclub he had been strikingly good-looking, in broad daylight, he was almost impossibly beautiful, sunlight glinting off his blue-black hair, lingering on cheekbones sharp as blades, a strong straight nose, a full wide mouth. And then those eyes, deeply densely dark, enhanced by lush black lashes yet disturbingly expressionless.

'Why unfortunately for me?' Maya queried.

'My father was probably the only *nice*—' he stressed the word with a sardonic twist of his mouth '—person in his family. I'm not nice and I have no ambition to be. You do, however, have something that I want, which I consider very providential for you in this scenario.'

'P-Providential?' she stammered, knocked off-balance by that unexpected statement because how could she possibly have anything that *he* could want?

'I have the power to make all the bad stuff in your life vanish,' Raffaele spelt out with blazing assurance. 'I know about *all* the debts your family have, so don't waste your time trying to bluff me. Now take a seat and we'll talk.'

His attitude set her teeth on edge, but she fought the sensation because, whether she liked it or not, he was the guy with the power. She settled down in an armchair in the seating area in the corner while he rang for coffee. It arrived at supersonic speed, on a tray carried by the receptionist, who didn't seem able to take her eyes off Raffaele. Like a mesmerised groupie she giggled when he spoke, and backed out again in a smiling daze as if she had touched liquid sunlight. Maya resisted the urge to roll her eyes, wondering if that was how women usually reacted to him, recalling how her own friends had behaved, and suppressed a sigh, wondering if she should ask what he had been doing in that club that night, wondering if it was wiser simply to leave the topic alone. But she didn't believe in a coincidence that far-fetched.

'So…tell me, why haven't you ditched your family yet?' Raffaele enquired as she took her first sip of coffee.

Maya almost choked and cleared her throat in haste, scanning him for a clue as to whether or not he was joking. He didn't look as if he was joking. 'Why would you ask me that?'

'It's an obvious question. Your family are like an albatross round your neck dragging you down,' Raffaele informed her. 'With your brain and your prospects, I would have ditched them long ago and moved on to make my own life.'

He was deadly serious. 'Your attitude tells me that you're not particularly close to your own family, because if you were you wouldn't need to be asking me that question,' Maya countered. 'I love them a great deal, even though they're flawed. But then nobody's perfect. I'm not either.'

'Your fatal flaw is that you're sentimental. I don't get attached to people,' Raffaele revealed, disconcerting her again.

'Why are we having this weird conversation?' she asked. 'I mean, we're strangers and this is supposed to be a business meeting.'

'How can we have a business meeting when I already know that you and your family are broke and completely unable to settle their debts? In that field, there is nothing to discuss. I don't waste time playing games for the sake of it.'

Maya sipped at her coffee, striving not to look at him, but somehow he commanded the room, drawing her attention continually back to his corner where he sat in a fluid sprawl of long limbs, a black tee stretched across his broad torso, faded, ripped and frayed designer denim clinging to long muscular thighs. Aware of where her gaze had strayed, she flushed, choosing in preference to focus on his lean bronzed face. 'You were in that club I was in, you approached me…

why?' she asked starkly, wishing that steady but uninformative dark regard of his weren't quite so unsettling.

'I wanted to see you in the flesh. I was curious. How up to date are you on our respective families' histories?'

'I know nothing about your family and only that my mother's family once wanted her to marry your father,' she admitted.

'Allow me to bring you up to speed,' Raffaele murmured, his concentration shot when she crossed her legs, revealing for a split second a tiny slice of pale inner thigh that was inexplicably outrageously erotic.

Raffaele clenched his strong jaw, questioning his libido's overreaction to such a tame glimpse of the female body. He didn't like how she turned him on hard and fast. He didn't like that he wanted to unbraid her hair to see it loose again and rip off that ugly suit and put her in clothing that would flatter her tall, slender figure. Such reactions didn't come naturally to him—at least they never had before with any other woman.

'You were saying,' she prompted, irritating him more.

He gave her a potted history of their families' marital misses and the news about her ancestor's will and the company. Her eyes widened. 'But that was really stupid of him... I mean, what if—?'

'Exactly,' Raffaele interposed. 'And all sorts of complications have arisen since with the company, particularly now that they have a dearth of Parisi talent to run it. It's going downhill and I want to acquire it.'

Maya glanced up, still mulling over the tangled tale he had spun. 'But you can't acquire it,' she said. 'Not without marrying and producing a child.'

'The mathematician can put two and two together.' Raffaele shifted his cup in a mocking congratulatory gesture. 'That's why you're here. You're my chance to buy.'

Maya was frowning, her incredulity rising in a great tide so that she set down her coffee cup and stood up, all flustered and defensive. 'And that's why you wanted to catch a look at me in the club,' she realised out loud. 'But I'm *not* your chance to buy the company... I couldn't marry you and have a child with you!'

'Never say never, Maya,' Raffaele advised with inhuman calm. 'Once you think it through, you'll realise that I'm offering you an unbeatable deal. Sit down again.'

'There's no reason for me to sit down again when I wouldn't even consider something so barbaric!' she exclaimed. 'And only a man very far removed from reality could label conceiving a child as an unbeatable *deal*!'

Raffaele angled his dark arrogant head back and smiled, startling her. 'There's the sentimental flaw coming out.'

'Don't you have *any* sense of decency?' Maya hissed down at him.

'Probably not but I do know that, while some women and men casually conceive kids on one-night stands, asking you to marry me *first* and have a child, whom I will fully support, is not that barbaric a request in today's world,' Raffaele maintained smoothly. 'If I have a child with you, it will probably be the only child I ever have and my heir, so you would be raising a child with every possible advantage and privilege from birth.'

'Money doesn't come into this equation. Right and wrong *do*!' Maya slammed back at him. 'Where's your conscience?'

'Where this issue is concerned it is as quiet as the grave,' Raffaele countered levelly. 'Your family is one step away from being put out on the street with a disabled child.'

'No, you really don't have a conscience,'

Maya decided, shocked by that reminder and trembling with the force of her emotions.

'Where has conscience got you dealing with your irresponsible father?' Raffaele enquired silkily. 'As a bonus, I would sort him out for you as well. He needs a job, not another business he can't cope with. You need to be realistic about the future. You can't save them from the consequences of their own stupidity all on your own. You *need* my money. *I* need a Parisi descendant as a wife and to have a child with.'

'You really are the most hateful man!' Maya slung at him wrathfully.

'And there's flaw number two,' Raffaele enumerated coolly. 'You're an emotional drama queen. I'm not an emotional person.'

'That's good,' Maya told him with a razor-edged smile as she snatched up the cream jug on the tray and doused him with what remained of the contents.

Raffaele vaulted upright, towering over her, his lean, devastatingly handsome features still calm and controlled as he shook himself as casually as a dog that had run through a puddle. 'Did that make you feel better, Maya?'

'Yes!' she yelled back at him as she stalked towards the door.

'But it hasn't changed the situation you're in, has it? So, you have some thinking to do,' Raffaele told her with infuriating cool. 'Walk round the block to dissipate the rage. Think *sensibly* about what I'm offering. I'm offering you your life back because I will free you from all responsibility for your family. All their debts will finally be settled. Their lives will only change for the better and so will yours because you won't have to worry about them any more.'

'Dear heaven, who did you take your lessons off? Svengali?' Maya gasped, her heart hammering, her head awash with murderous impulses she had never experienced in her life before. She was so enraged that she was shaking all over.

'I'm more Machiavellian in outlook,' Raffaele paused to tell her gravely. 'You need to take a deep breath and count to ten before you try to deal with me because losing your temper will back you into a corner and ensure that you lose every time.'

'I would sooner *die* than be married to a monster like you!' Maya shouted at him.

'I don't think so, Maya. I think you'll be back here within the hour with a different attitude because I'm the only option you have right now,' Raffaele forecast with a satisfaction that blazed like a neon sign in his scorching dark golden eyes.

Just when she had decided he was a sociopath he'd revealed an emotion, only not the right kind of emotion, while he had reduced her to a mindless state of rage. Had she ever pictured herself burying a knife in a man's chest before? She didn't think so. In a daze she stalked back out and into the lift. She couldn't think straight.

Raffaele immediately got on the phone to Sal to instruct that one of his bodyguards should tail her.

'Why?' Sal asked baldly.

'She's in shock. I don't want her stepping out in front of a bus…or something,' Raffaele murmured. 'Not when she's going to be my wife.'

'She *agreed*?' Sal demanded.

'She will,' Raffaele confirmed with unblemished confidence.

Without any idea where she was going, Maya marched down the street as though she was on a mission. Her brain was awash with conflicting thoughts laced with a depth of anger she hadn't known she had the ability to feel.

He had asked her to conceive a baby as part of a business *deal*, apparently quite content to create his own flesh and blood purely in the name of profit, recognising nothing wrong in such behaviour. What a poor little mite that child would be! He was immoral, unscrupulous and totally free of normal civilised constraints, as if he had been reared in a jungle well away from the rest of the human race. She had never met anyone that avant-garde before and he had shocked her to her conservative core. When her feet began to ache in her cheap but presentable black medium-heel shoes she walked into a café and bought a cup of tea.

As the sheer shock value of meeting with Raffaele Manzini ebbed, realities began flocking back in to weigh her down. Just as *he* had forecast, which sent another spear of fury rattling through her slim body. It was pointless to have become so angry when she was powerless, she recognised, ready to kick herself for being so impressionable. She had been traumatised by his shamelessly insouciant suggestion that she go to bed with him to have a baby to allow *him* to acquire a company he wanted. Did he honestly believe that a wedding ring would take away the shock of that proposition? Could any guy be more cold-blooded?

Yet suddenly she was trapped in a corner with an offer of a rescue that had come out of left field at her when she had least expected it. He had spelt out what he would do for her family. He had been blunt. He would settle *all* the debts, an almost unimaginable concept to Maya, who had been struggling for so long and for so many years to keep those debts at bay and protect her family. And then Raffaele Manzini came along, evidently wealthy enough to the point where money could be flung around wastefully because her family was *deep* in debt and it would take an enormous amount to settle what they owed.

Seemingly he could afford it. Who *was* Raffaele Manzini? She looked him up on her phone and broke out in goosebumps when she found out. He was *so* rich he belonged to the tribe of the super-rich. What her family owed would barely be pocket change for him. In fact, in asking her to marry him he was scraping the bottom of the barrel because he was a man who appeared to inhabit an exclusive world featuring crowned heads and oil-rich billionaires. But then he was only asking her because her mother had been born a Parisi.

Who she was, what she was, were immaterial facts to him because it *wasn't* personal to him, it was simply business.

And he had put her in a quandary because she was clever enough to accept that he had given her the only choice she was likely to be given. It was a choice between marrying Raffaele Manzini and her family being made bankrupt and homeless. There was no compassion in him. He wanted what he wanted and to hell with who else got hurt in the process, she reasoned angrily, momentarily overpowered by the idea of having to deal with someone that far removed from her in moral outlook.

Women had had to do worse things in tight corners than marry and reproduce, she told herself fiercely. Oh, how she hated the reality that *he* had foreseen that she would change her mind! How could she marry someone she didn't even like or admire? How could she go to bed with him? Give him a child? In a rush she suppressed those reactions, which now felt embarrassingly weak and *sentimental*. Best not to think about those things, she told herself firmly, determined to reclaim her peace of mind and take a rational view of the situation. It would be much wiser to take it all one step at a time and handle events as they happened.

Raffaele Manzini was offering her family an escape route into a new way of life, a safer, more stable life such as they had *never* enjoyed before. After all, the crash of the very first business her father had started up was still following him with debts twenty years later. It would take so much stress off her parents; best of all it would protect her little brother, Matt, from the consequences of bankruptcy and homelessness. And Raffaele might think it was stupid for her to love her family as much as she did but what did that matter to her? There were no loving grandparents or any other relatives for her family to turn to in a crisis. Izzy, her twin, always tried to help but there wasn't much more she could do. There *was* only Maya and, like it or not, her family *needed* her. And if she could give them that one perfect chance to start afresh with a clean sheet, wouldn't that be the most wonderful gift for the *whole* family?

It wasn't as though she didn't like babies either. She adored babies but she couldn't even imagine having a child with Raffaele Manzini. *You're not allowed to think about the mechanics of the production project*, she reminded herself fiercely. Panic would plunge her back into emotional mode and that got her nowhere. Although he *was* a cold-blooded, callous, four-letter word of a guy to have confronted her as he had, both in the club and in that office.

Don't think about that either, she told herself firmly. If she had to say yes, it was more sensible not to dwell on any of it except in so far as she would have to protect herself in every way possible, she reasoned, tugging out a notebook and beginning to make rapid notes of certain non-negotiable demands she would have to make on her own behalf.

An hour after that Maya was walking back into Manzini Finance. Although she felt cool and in control, she knew it wouldn't last once she was exposed to *him* again. He put her on edge, he outraged her, he continually hogged the drivers' seat. Well, not *this* time around, she decided, wearing a steely expression that none of her family would have recognised.

CHAPTER THREE

'IT TOOK YOU a little longer to get up to speed than I expected,' Raffaele drawled cuttingly, surveying Maya with the complacent look of a cat with a cornered mouse. 'But here we are again.'

'Yes, here we are,' Maya agreed flat in tone, head held high, fingernails biting into her palms viciously because he hadn't been able to resist needling her even though he had won and that told her a lot about Raffaele Manzini. Resistance inflamed him because he wasn't accustomed to having to handle it, but he was going to *have* to learn because intelligence warned her that she and Raffaele were oil and water and would fight every step of the way.

'Take a seat,' he intoned smoothly.

'Don't mind if I do.' Maya settled back into the seat she had vacated in her rage earlier.

'I'll get straight to the point. I don't like you. I don't like anything I've so far seen in you but, as you said, you're the only game in town. If I want to help my family out of a crisis, I don't have a choice.'

'Oh, don't come over all martyr on me, Maya, because it's untrue,' Raffaele sliced in icily, wondering if anyone had ever dared to tell him that they didn't like him before, knowing they hadn't while wondering why that single tiny opinion should sting. 'If you do this, you do it by your *own* choice, not anyone else's.'

Hatred lashed through Maya like a storm unfurling inside her chest and that quickly she wanted to assault him again, because it was as if she were Eve in the Garden of Eden and he wouldn't even allow her a fig leaf to hide behind, no, not even the smallest excuse. 'Right, I do it by my own choice,' she gritted. 'But there are conditions.'

'I set the conditions.'

'No, you can't set *all* of them,' Maya countered steadily. 'I'm entitled to certain safeguards. The first is exclusivity. You stay out of other women's beds while you're with me.'

Raffaele's head flung up and back in surprise, luxuriant tousled black hair tumbling back from his cliff-edge cheekbones, dark eyes awash with gold rebellion. 'No.'

'I am not sleeping with you while you also sleep with other women,' Maya told him curtly. 'That is non-negotiable. If you can't commit to that, then we'll have to use artificial insemination as our method of conception.'

For a split second, Raffaele could not credit that she had said that to him because, in response, *hell no* flared straight through his every skin cell like an alarm bell, firing up his tension because he already knew that he wanted her. No, artificial insemination wasn't an acceptable alternative for him... even though he felt as though it *should've* been? That he shouldn't be so sexually invested in her in what was basically a business deal? So, he was human, after all, he reminded himself wryly.

'That's a yes to exclusivity but, once you're pregnant, all bets are off,' Raffaele conceded, choosing to be reasonable when he himself least felt like being reasonable because there was something about her that continually scratched him the wrong way and made him feel ridiculously like a rebellious teenager.

'That will do…' Almost imperceptibly, Maya's slender body lost some of its tension.

'Fidelity means *that* much to you?' Raffaele shot at her in surprise. 'I've never been faithful to anyone, but then I've never had anyone close enough to be faithful to.'

'As far as I'm concerned fidelity is the bedrock of any relationship.'

'I haven't *had* a relationship with a woman before,' Raffaele clarified without the smallest hint of discomfiture in making that admission. 'I have sexual affairs that rarely last longer than a couple of weeks.'

'That kind of shallow is just a touch adolescent at your age,' Maya remarked.

Raffaele was incredulous when he felt the hit of heat striking his cheekbones. He could not recall when anyone had last embarrassed him. His dark eyes flared bright as gold ingots with anger. 'I've always preferred to steer clear of serious relationships,' he told her.

'I read your profile online. That was kind of obvious. Right, moving on,' Maya continued with an air of efficiency that exasperated him. 'Health screening. That has to be done.'

'I don't have unprotected sex.'

'But you will be having it with me and if

I agree to getting tested, you can too,' Maya cut in.

Raffaele spoke through gritted teeth. 'Anything else you feel as though you must air?'

'Yes, what do we do if a pregnancy doesn't happen? It can take up to a year even for a healthy couple to conceive. Were you aware of that?'

No, actually he hadn't been, but he would have preferred flogging to admitting that salient fact to her! Raffaele knew absolutely nothing about conception or pregnancy, only how best to *avoid* that development, which was why he had never taken the tiniest risk in that field.

'We can only deal with that situation if it occurs,' Raffaele fielded impatiently.

'I want full custody of any child we may have,' Maya informed him next.

'I won't agree to anything other than joint custody. For all I know you'll be a terrible mother,' Raffaele responded. 'I will maintain access rights to any child we have for that reason. It's my duty to protect my child too.'

Maya blinked in surprise, disconcerted by his attitude because she had fully expected him to be willing to sign over any rights to that prospective child whom he only wanted in the first place to fulfil a business purpose. That he should actually care about the child's welfare was a plus in his favour, the only plus he had shown her so far, she acknowledged grudgingly.

'Where is all this conception stuff to take place?' she enquired, pleased by her calmness.

'Italy, where we'll get married. I'm already putting the arrangements in order,' Raffaele volunteered.

Maya stiffened. 'You *do* like to put the cart before the horse, don't you?'

'But then I knew you'd come down off *your* high horse and agree,' Raffaele replied, setting her teeth on edge again.

'We'll be living in Italy?' she questioned. 'What am I supposed to tell my family?'

Raffaele shrugged a broad shoulder with magnificent disdain. 'Tell them we're getting married? You don't need to tell the whole truth. You could spin a love-at-first-sight story.'

'I don't like telling lies,' Maya said icily. 'I'll tell them you've offered me a job in Italy and that because of that famously compassionate streak of yours—' her lip curled at that provocative phrase and his teeth clenched again '—you've decided to erase their debts because of the connection that once existed between our families.'

'The *hate* connection, you mean?' A rough-edged laugh parted Raffaele's perfect masculine lips. 'Tell them whatever you like. It's not my business.'

'But you *made* it your business. You own *all* their debts, don't you? It's too big a coincidence that all their debts came home to roost on the same day,' Maya opined in disgust.

Raffaele jerked his chin in unashamed acknowledgement.

'So, you set up me up for this…*literally*,' Maya accused.

'No, you can thank my great-grandfather, Aldo, rather than me for that move. I didn't know you existed until he made me aware of it before informing me that he owned your family lock, stock and barrel,' Raffaele recounted drily. 'If I hadn't been willing to play ball and go for the deal he offered me, he would have happily bankrupted your parents and made them homeless because he has no reason to like your family.'

An angry smile tilted Maya's lush pink mouth. 'Are you implying that I should be grateful for you and the marriage proposal?'

'*Sì*...' Raffaele confirmed, golden flames dancing in his arrogant challenging gaze. 'Without me, where would you and your family be?'

Incensed afresh, Maya jumped up. 'You just couldn't be kind for even ten minutes, could you be?' she snapped back at him, her furious voice shaking. 'You want me on my knees in gratitude...don't you?'

A sudden disturbing grin flashed across his lean, devastatingly handsome features as he vaulted upright, towering over her with his superior height. 'Now you're talking my language...what I wouldn't give at this moment to have you there!'

The explicit image she assumed he intended struck her like a mortifying, humiliating blow as she belatedly realised what she had said, and it was too much on top of everything else she had already endured from him. Her hand flashed up and he caught her wrist between long brown fingers before the slap could connect, his reflexes far faster than her own. 'No, don't you *dare*!' he breathed in a raw, wrathful undertone. 'Nobody hits me now.'

Nobody hits me now? What on earth did he mean? For an instant, Maya froze in shock and bewilderment at what he had said and what she had almost done. She was on the very brink of apologising as she moved away in a blindly direct line with the corner of the coffee table when he simply stretched down his long arms and scooped her up from the other side of the table separating them and lifted her bodily into the air. 'I'm sorry...put me down!' she gasped.

'I'm not going to hurt you. I don't *hurt* women. You were about to trip over the table,' Raffaele bit out, almost breathless as he stared down into her bright green eyes and his scorching gaze trailed down her heart-shaped face to the pillowy invitation of her pink lips. A raging beast of sexual hunger was clawing at him, disorientating him. *Nobody* hits *me now?* Why the hell had he let that slip out? He never, ever referred to the abuse he had suffered as a child.

'That's good, and thanks...now put me down,' Maya repeated urgently, her heart hammering so hard inside her chest she thought it might jump right out.

After an instant of hesitation during which she believed he was not about to listen to her at all, Raffaele slowly lowered her back to the floor a safe distance from the table and she snatched in a gasping breath. 'I didn't intend to frighten you,' he said flatly.

'I wasn't frightened, not exactly,' Maya framed, all out of breath and inspiration because, for the count of the ten seconds he had held her, she had experienced panic and then the strangest inner pulse of excitement that had left her quivering and embarrassed and all over the place. 'I'm sorry I went for you like that. You made me very angry. That's not an excuse...well, it is, isn't it? But I have never tried to hit another person before in my life and it won't happen again, I assure you.'

'Forget it,' Raffaele advised carelessly, fighting to suppress the sexual arousal she induced, willing away the desire pushing against his zipper, yes, the thought of her on her knees half-naked, yes, that really pressed every one of his sexual triggers and filled him with lust. 'But, as it looks like we're going to have a confrontational relationship, it makes sense to start working on that problem now.'

'*Now?*' Still a little dazed from dealing with him, simply being trapped in his energising, maddening radius, Maya looked up at him, her face feeling as flushed as though she had a fever.

'Yes, now. Time you started adapting to

me and I start adapting to you because we're going to have to live together, potentially for months,' Raffaele pointed out levelly. 'We'll go and get you some clothes and we'll go out tonight.'

'Get me clothes?' she echoed in bewilderment.

'I hate that rag of a suit. I'll pick clothing for you and we'll go out,' Raffaele repeated, shooting her an assessing appraisal. 'This is your new life, Maya. *Show* me that you can handle it.'

Maya swallowed hard and just nodded, wondering what was wrong with her brain because it seemed to have gone to sleep. He wanted proof that she could act normally and fit into his world and she couldn't blame him for that. Was buying women clothes something he was used to doing?

Half an hour later, she was in a beauty salon, having her hair done and her nails painted, and her face made up. It was like a television makeover except with Raffaele in charge, his opinions sought, rather than hers. And she let him do it, reminding herself of what he would do for her family. He would take the nightmare of debt away. Surely it was a small enough sacrifice in return for her to surrender her independence and her strong will? But she'd never done the feminine stuff before, had never really cared what she wore or how she looked as long as she was decently covered.

Two hours later still, she was standing on a dais in a designer salon, clad in garments she wouldn't have been caught dead in and congratulating herself on her self-discipline in not fighting him. It disconcerted her, though, that Raffaele could be so determined to transform her at what she imagined to be enormous expense into the kind of woman he obviously preferred.

'That'll do,' he eventually conceded, beautiful wilful mouth still down-turning even after about the twentieth outfit that had been tried on for his perusal.

Raffaele didn't know why he was still so dissatisfied with Maya's appearance. Logically, she looked beautiful, hair like a pale shimmering veil loose to her waist, face enhanced with subtle cosmetics, glorious legs exposed in a brocade skirt that was the sort of thing he had seen other women wear. The leather and lace corset top exposed her delicate shoulders and slender arms, her pale, smooth, flawless skin exercising the most weird allure for him—he wanted to see his own hands on that skin with a hunger that was beginning to seriously annoy him because it wasn't cool. But she still didn't look *right* and why would she, he asked himself sarcastically, when he had never in his life before taken it upon himself to choose clothing for a woman?

And why had he done it? The power trip? He couldn't deny the appeal of that aspect. She brought out a bone-deep dominant urge he hadn't known he even possessed. But one look at her had also warned him that *she* didn't have a clue how to dress and surely he could not do worse with that challenge than she already had? In fact, he didn't think she had the slightest interest in what she put on her body because not once…and he had been watching carefully…had she demonstrated even a spark of pleasure at the vast choice of clothing now open to her. And he had watched her grimace at her make-up–enhanced features in the mirror, seemingly indifferent to how beautiful she looked. Didn't she have any normal female traits? Where was her vanity? Her drive to look her best? To impress? Even if it was only to impress other women?

Well, she *still* wasn't looking to impress him, he acknowledged grimly. Shopping, while being a pastime guaranteed to thrill most women, with Maya was like taking a robot out. She behaved as if she had resolved to do whatever it took to satisfy him while remaining determined not to take the smallest ounce of personal enjoyment out of the experience. Her vital spark was missing and it annoyed him. It *hugely* annoyed him. He might have told her that they needed to work on their confrontational vibe but, in truth, he enjoyed that vibe. No woman had ever come back at him as Maya did, refusing to please, refusing to accept her place, refusing to flatter his ego.

'You look good,' he told her almost fiercely.

Maya stepped daintily off the dais in the flamboyantly high heels he had insisted on. 'Well, you can tell what sort of women you're used to,' she commented half under her breath.

'Educate me,' Raffaele urged.

'Isn't it obvious? A skirt too short and tight to sit down in comfortably? Shoes I have to totter in? A top that bares far too much flesh?'

'You're not endowed enough in that sector to be showing too much flesh,' Raffaele riposted.

Maya hitched a naked little shoulder. 'So sorry if I am a disappointment in any department,' she murmured with a tiny poisonous smile.

'Sadly for you,' Raffaele retorted deadpan, resting a big bronzed hand possessively on a slim shoulder, 'you are *exactly* what I like most.'

'Cheap looking,' Maya said, tossing him a mutinous glance.

And disturbingly, Raffaele laughed with rich appreciation and resisted the urge to ask the designer hovering for an opinion because she wasn't likely to diss her own designs. He did not go for cheap-looking women...*did he*? Certainly, nobody could have accused him of going for unadventurous types, he conceded. Possibly he had always instinctively sought out the wilder, freer women, least likely to seek anything other than a bout of exciting sex from him.

No, Maya didn't fit the mould, but if he toned himself down a little and she relaxed a little, they could meet somewhere in the middle, couldn't they? *Madonna mia*... Thunderstruck at the sudden realisation that he

was toying with the idea of changing his behaviour to *please* a woman, Raffaele froze
in fleeting consternation. No, that was the
wrong reading of the situation, he reasoned
speedily. He might never have been in a relationship before, but he was required to make
that effort with Maya to attain his ultimate
goal. He was engaged in an act of persuasion
aimed at coaxing Maya into accepting the
necessary status quo. *Sì*, that sounded much
more like him…calculating and logical.

He took her to a private members' club for
dinner. She walked like a queen through the
public dining room into the private room he
had engaged. A momentary hush fell on their
entry. Every eye was on her as diners greeted
him with nods and waves, but she looked at
no one, little chin held high, clear green eyes
blank. He had seen models on catwalks with
more expression. It foiled him: he couldn't
tell what she was thinking, and why was that
annoying too?

Her slender neck looked bare: she needed
jewellery. He recalled his mother's vast cache
of jewels stowed in a bank vault since her
death and he thought, why not let Maya wear
them? They were unlikely to be worn again in
his lifetime because he didn't ever see himself

taking a wife for real. Maya wouldn't be able to keep the jewellery, of course. He would get that written into the pre-nup already being drawn up for them. He stabbed a button on his phone, speaking to his Italian lawyer as they were ushered to their table.

Maya collapsed down with relief into a chair, flexing her crushed toes in the new shoes, wondering if she dared to slip them off, would she ever get them on again to walk out? Going out with Raffaele was an educational experience, she mused dizzily. People dropped everything to attend to his needs. He had walked into a beauty salon with a busy waiting area and she had been led straight to a stylist. In the same manner, the designer had abandoned someone else to deal with her needs exclusively.

Raffaele was richer than rich, and businesspeople knew it and fawned on him, granting his every demand without protest or delay. No doubt he paid in spades for that kind of service but being in the presence of the power that extreme wealth gave him over others was shocking in its own way, and had taught Maya why he hadn't expected her to argue with anything. He was much more accustomed to those slavishly eager to please, ready to roll over and perform obediently at his first request.

'How do you know so much about me and my family?' Maya enquired over the first course.

'Aldo gave me a file,' Raffaele admitted. 'That's how he does business. He still has a bee in his bonnet about the fact that his grandson, my father, gave your parents the money to set up home in the UK.'

'And it *was* given, not loaned, according to my parents,' Maya cut in curtly.

'But it was Aldo's cash,' Raffaele retorted with finality. 'My father cut ties with his family soon afterwards when he married my mother instead of yours as Aldo had decreed.'

'So, Aldo is bossy like you,' Maya observed.

'I'm not bossy.'

'You *so* are,' Maya told him, lifting a fine blonde brow in emphasis.

Raffaele could feel his patience sliding again. 'Let's leave how we arrived at this point behind us. They're not *your* debts.'

'But I'm the one paying for them,' she pointed out helplessly.

'This topic is closed,' Raffaele dictated.

Silence fell. Maya dealt him an amused glance and concentrated on her food.

'Possibly…' Raffaele breathed tautly. 'I can be a little too dominant.'

'Or…' Maya pondered. 'You just want to leave the truth behind and make me behave like I'm one of your women.'

'I do not have women in the plural,' Raffaele informed her levelly. 'Why are you so determined to argue with me?'

A faint pink lit Maya's face and she jerked a slight shoulder and fell silent. She felt an intense need to keep him at a distance. Because she disliked him? Or because dredging her attention from that lean, beautiful face of his across the table was becomingly increasingly difficult? This close he had stunning eyes, dark pools laced with fascinating gold highlights, inky black lashes even better than eyeliner at framing that lustrous gaze. Her breath feathered in her throat, her chest tightening as she felt her nipples stiffen, and a hollow ache stirred between her thighs. She was not so dumb that she didn't know what was happening to her even if it hadn't happened to her in a man's company before…

It struck her as cruelly ironic that that surge of physical attraction should strike with Raffaele Manzini. She had been waiting, *wanting* to feel that exciting hormonal buzz with a man and take advantage of it to gain some sexual experience. Her face bloomed with colour because that seemed such an obnoxious thought to have, but as it dawned on her that Raffaele Manzini would be her first lover she found herself wishing that she weren't still a virgin. No man had ever drawn her enough to want to take that final step. Was that why she had been waiting like the Sleeping Beauty, or some such silly creature, for that first love to come along and give her that happy fairy-tale ending?

She almost laughed at how ridiculously naïve she had been for so many years, honestly believing that that one very special guy was going to just magically appear for her. That wasn't how life worked. Life wasn't that neat and tidy; it wasn't like an exam to prepare for and pass. But Maya had never done anything she hadn't pre-planned because she rarely took risks, had learned at far too early an age that she was the one who had to be mature, sensible and careful to look after her family. There had been no teenaged crushes, no infatuations, no first boyfriend who counted in any meaningful way. The whole sex and romance story had passed her by while she'd worked and studied and passed exam after exam because the academic world was stable and sensible and gave her no nasty surprises.

And it was a very nasty surprise to accept that she could feel her body burn as though someone had turned a blowtorch on her just because a man smiled. Raffaele Manzini, womaniser that he was, had dynamite sex appeal. It had nothing to do with her brain, it was all physical, meaningless, forgettable, she told herself urgently. He was making conversation, smoothly, entertainingly, sticking slickly to the impersonal because she knew that he had decided that *she* was prickly and difficult. But she wasn't, she *wasn't*. He…he just made her angry. And why was he surprised by that when he had virtually blackmailed her into agreeing to marry him and have a child for him? Was he so spoiled by her sex that, no matter what he did, he expected admiration and appreciation?

'I was planning to take you to a club *but* I think you'd prefer to go home.'

'I would but not dressed like this,' Maya confessed. 'I'll tell my family lies tomorrow, not tonight. I'm too tired this evening to tell smiling, soothing lies.'

'I'll take you back to my apartment to change. Your clothes are there,' Raffaele admitted.

'Why are they at your apartment?' Maya asked as she stood up, wincing as she forced her feet back into the new shoes again.

'Obviously because I thought you'd spend the night with me,' Raffaele confessed without hesitation. 'Why would we wait for a ring to get this show on the road?'

Even in her heels she had to tilt her head to look up at him. He had to be six feet four or five. His confession had blown her resolve to be polite and pleasant right out of the water again because it told her so much that she didn't want to see in him. 'You are unbelievable,' she snapped at him, bristling with distaste. 'I only met you properly for the first time this morning!'

'Believe me, it feels like I've known you a lot longer,' Raffaele murmured, sincere for once because he couldn't quite credit that it had only been a few hours since their first meeting. In the strangest way, in a way he couldn't possibly explain, he felt ridiculously comfortable with Maya even though she had sat there damning him with her eyes and acting moody as hell.

But Maya was only winding up, her temper like petrol on a bonfire as she studied his ridiculously beautiful and insouciant face. 'And you thought I would be willing to fall into bed with you *immediately*?' She gasped incredulously.

'A guy can hope—that's not a crime,' Raffaele fielded, shifting to ease the pressure on his jeans because there it was again, that spear of unholy lust that she roused without even *trying*, without even touching him. The sexual charge of her blew him away.

'You don't hope, you *expect*!' Maya corrected angrily, gathering her bag in a quick angry movement and clutching it to her chest. 'Sex and baby-making is off the table *until* we're married.'

'That doesn't surprise me.'

Maya stalked forward, green eyes bright as emeralds. 'Why doesn't it surprise you?'

'Because you don't trust me, you don't trust anyone,' Raffaele told her softly. 'I'm like that too. And on top of not trusting, you're…inhibited.'

'I'm not inhibited!' Maya snapped at him.

Raffaele took her hand and pressed her back against the wall. 'If you're not, kiss me.'

'I'm not kissing you!' Maya spat.

'But secretly you know you want to,' Raffaele purred, leaning down to steal a tiny kiss from her pink pouting mouth, lingering to nibble on her full soft lower lip, sending a shattering flood of sensation snaking right down into her pelvis. 'One kiss…that's all… I promise not to try to take it any further.'

'OK…one kiss,' Maya conceded in a deliberately bored tone. 'Then you let go of me and you *don't* forget about those *health* checks.'

He kissed her and the world fell away. She hadn't believed that could happen, but it did. Her fear surged beneath the drowning electrifying pleasure that consumed her when his tongue licked against hers, unexpectedly subtle, incredibly sexy in technique, like nothing she had ever experienced before in her life, and for the first time ever she wanted more, arms travelling round him, hands smoothing over a broad, warm, strong back before sliding down to curve to lean hips.

'I won't forget about the health checks,' Raffaele breathed, lifting his head, dark eyes flaming bright as the sun with hunger. 'Stay the night with me,' he urged. 'I'll use protection.'

Maya returned to planet earth again, unnerved by his physical effect on her, trembling, all hot and flustered in a way she wasn't used to being. 'No, thanks. I want to go home, please,' she said as tightly as a little girl trying to show that she could be polite even in trying circumstances.

'Stay the night with me. I'll use protection.'

Raffaele had knocked her straight back down to reality again. Nothing romantic or special there, she mocked herself for the quivering hunger still tugging at her unrepentant body. Raffaele was just like all the other men she had met, wanting more what he couldn't have. Reluctance only heightened her appeal with such men.

'As you wish...' Raffaele gritted his teeth. 'But I don't understand you.'

'Of course, you don't. I'm not the type of woman you're used to,' Maya pointed out drily as she opened the door to leave. 'I'm not anyone's one-night stand.'

Raffaele breathed in so deep that he thought the top of his head ought to go flying off. 'We're getting married within the next week.'

Beneath his disbelieving gaze, Maya grimaced. 'I wasn't expecting it to be quite *that* soon—'

'Let's move,' Raffaele urged, planting a hand to her rigid spine, watching male heads turn to watch her progress, those endless perfect legs, that shimmering cloud of naturally fair hair. The whole time he was thinking, She may not know it yet but *she's mine*, will be absolutely totally mine. He marvelled at that thought, smiled with amusement at it, could not get over quite how invested he was becoming in the project to acquire her grandparents' company.

CHAPTER FOUR

RAFFAELE LIVED IN a breathtaking penthouse apartment with a fabulous view of London at night.

Maya, concentrating on the need to escape his company, spared it barely a glance, wincing in her tight shoes as she walked down a tiled corridor to the bedroom he had indicated and shutting the door firmly in his lean bronzed face.

Kicking off the shoes with relief, she scrambled to get into her own clothes again and walked into the adjoining bathroom to do what she could to scrub off the cosmetics she rarely wore. She did not want her family to suspect anything was amiss. Luckily, she had not yet got around to mentioning the job she had already found in London and she would tell them instead that she had got a fabulous job in Italy with Raffaele Manzini. Her story would all tie in nicely together then, with Raffaele starring as the kind and generous guy he, most certainly, wasn't. By the time she finished telling them that he was also writing off their debts, her parents would be extravagantly happy, and it was many months since she had seen them in that state and she couldn't wait to see their faces. That was the pay-off, she reminded herself firmly, her family's security and contentment would be her reward for what she was doing but, no, she wasn't planning to act the martyr even inside her own head.

But she didn't feel the same about lying to her sister because she had never lied to her sister before; she'd possibly told the odd fib to save Izzy from hurt feelings but never anything more than that because, as twins, they were so close. She winced, reckoning that this time around she didn't have much choice.

Raffaele felt a little like he had as a child when he had tried to capture a summer dandelion clock floating through the air and signally failed. He didn't understand Maya. She didn't *like* him. She might be as hungry for him as he was for her, but she wouldn't break even *one* of her doubtless lengthy list of rules to have him. For that reason and for the unavoidable truth that Maya's liking and acceptance were important to him for the foreseeable future, he would make an effort with a woman for the first time in his life, only there was just one small problem: he hadn't a clue *how* to do that. He frowned, exasperated by the uncharacteristic uncertainty engulfing him.

'What sort of clothes do I like?' Maya echoed dimly, several days later, stretching back on her bunk bed with her phone cradled close. 'I've never really thought much about it. Students only dress for important interviews. I like elegant and feminine, not fussy and frilly, though, and never ever short, tight or revealing. Why on earth are you asking?'

'I have a wedding dress to choose since you said you don't care what you wear.'

'I wasn't being awkward,' Maya said apologetically, wondering why she got on with Raffaele so much better on the phone than she did in person. 'I mean…it's not a *real* wedding, that's what I meant.'

'But we want it to *look* real,' Raffaele countered. 'Aldo's coming, so are some of my friends.'

That was all news to Maya, and it disconcerted her. 'Oh…er…well—'

'Want to join me today?' Raffaele pressed.
'You could pick your own dress.'

His dark deep voice purred down her spine
like a caress and she rolled her eyes at the
thought. He had rung her every day, asked
her out every day while chattering about completely inconsequential things. What on earth
was he playing at? Why was he bothering?
What nefarious purpose was his uncharacteristic niceness supposed to achieve for him?

'I'm taking my brother out to the British
Museum…sorry—' She would have loved to
see her sister, Izzy, but knew that would be
unwise with all that was going on and the fic-
tions she had had to tell her family. Besides,
Izzy had gone strangely quiet herself recently.

'You spent yesterday with him as well,'
Raffaele reminded her with an edge.

'I'm going to be parted from my family
for months.'

'I've already assured you that you can fly
home and visit them any time you want. It's
all in the pre-nuptial agreement. Didn't you
read it?'

'I read it cover to cover.' Maya set her teeth
together before she found herself arguing

with him again about the allowance he was insisting she would receive after their marriage terminated, and the even bigger fortune she would walk away with should they have a child. It all seemed so cold and dry and shoddy to her, raised as she had been to look on marriage and child-bearing as something you only did with someone you loved. Only she could hardly say that to Raffaele when she had agreed to those terms, could she?

Maya's breath caught in her throat when she saw the sprawling mansion at the foot of the long straight drive. Somehow she had expected Raffaele's home in Tuscany to be as aggressively modern as his London apartment, and the big graceful property with its landscaped gardens and much older design took her by surprise. Whatever, it scarcely mattered to her, she reasoned apprehensively when her wedding was only a few hours away, to be staged that very afternoon.

How could she possibly be getting married without a single member of her family present? And how could she be marrying a man she didn't love? A kind of panic Maya had never felt before sat like a large immovable stone in her hollow tummy. That panic had nothing to do with logic and had not even been soothed by her family's display of happy relief that week as her parents were freed from all their worst fears and were finally able to contemplate a fresh start in life. Her father, Rory, was actually looking for a job, admitting to her that he had only kept on trying to start up his own business because he had believed that a successful business was his only hope of amassing sufficient cash to pay off their debts.

But, worst of all, Maya missed her twin sister, because Izzy had always been her safe place when the cruel realities of life threatened to crush her. She was used to confiding in Izzy, being soothed by her sibling's more light-hearted and optimistic nature. But she could *not* share her current predicament with Izzy, because she knew that Izzy would've told her not to go ahead, and that their parents' financial problems were not solely their responsibility to fix. Unfortunately, the hard truth of that belief, Maya acknowledged ruefully, was that there *was* nobody else to fix those problems, and that watching poor little Matt suffer alongside their parents was more than Maya could bear when she had been put in a position where she could help. For that reason, there was no excuse for distressing her twin with a situation that could not be changed by wishful thinking. She would tell her sister afterwards, when the whole wretched arrangement was almost over... perhaps once she had conceived.

Of course, that wasn't something she could think about when conception was inextricably linked to the necessity of having sex with Raffaele Manzini. He was gorgeous. Doubtless he would be charming and experienced and pretty much physically what the average woman could only dream of for her first experience. But what mattered most to Maya was that she had no sense of connection with him. Her body operated around him on its own agenda while her brain stayed free, recognising the cold calculation in him, the ruthlessness, the lack of caring. He could flirt, he could talk up a storm, in truth he could be incredibly entertaining, but it wasn't enough for her...

Only it *had* to be enough, she reminded herself doggedly as she climbed out of the limo that had brought her from the airport, fresh from the incredible luxury of her flight in the Manzini private jet. And now it was her wedding day and she had to settle down and accept the conditions she had already agreed, she told herself urgently. Deep down inside she was far too sensitive, far too much of a dreamer, *weak*, she thought, full of self-loathing at that moment. With Raffaele, she needed to be tough as steel and hard as stone to hold her own.

Raffaele watched her emerge from the limo, a slender graceful figure in jeans and a light top, blonde hair braided down her back, and that fast his body reacted. He was amused because that reaction was only telling him what he already knew: Maya had a weird effect on him. The sound of her husky laughter on the phone affected him the same strange way. He only hoped that she would be pleased with the surprise he had helped to engineer for her. Surely she would be delighted? Nobody appeared to be more family-orientated than Maya was.

Maya was disconcerted to find Raffaele poised in the grand hallway. Her luggage was being ferried past her while a maid waited to show her upstairs to her room. A smile curved his shapely sculpted lips and, for once, carried up to lighten his dark eyes to shimmering gold, and her heart stuttered as though he had punched her, she reflected with inner recoil at her response to him. Posed there in sunlight, blue-black hair gleaming, his flawless bronzed features smiling, and his tall, powerful physique casually clad in jeans and a tee, he took her breath away...whether she liked it or not.

'I have a surprise for you. I can only hope it's a good one,' Raffaele murmured quietly. 'Your grandparents are here, hoping to meet you.'

'My... P-Parisi grandparents?' Maya stammered in disbelief.

'Aldo told them about the wedding, and they contacted me to ask if they could attend. They're a little disappointed that your mother and your siblings won't be coming but they're very eager to meet you,' he told her.

'But I thought they wanted nothing to do with any of us!' she exclaimed, taken aback by the development but wondering only briefly how to behave because she had been raised to always be polite and kind.

'I think you'll find that the passage of time and loneliness have changed their outlook. Your mother *is* an only child,' Raffaele reminded her. 'But be warned, your grandmother cries a lot. She's very emotional.'

'So is my mother,' Maya confided with a

sudden smile as she braced herself because Raffaele already had a hand at her spine to press her into the room.

Maya focused on the two people who had stood up to greet her. They were older than she had expected, must have been quite an age when her mother was born, she worked out, searching their faces for familiarity and finding it there in her grandmother's damp dark eyes and her small, portly grandfather's anxious expression. She could see her mother's lineage in their faces, and it warmed her into moving forward and extending her arms to the weeping older woman.

'Maya, this is Fortunato and Assunta Parisi, your grandparents,' Raffaele told her.

'I am your *nonna*,' the elderly lady framed on the back of a sob.

'I'll leave you to get acquainted,' Raffaele volunteered, closing the door again.

And there was much chatter and many tears from Maya's *nonna* as the older woman looked in delight at the photos on Maya's phone to see the daughter she had not seen for over twenty years and the pictures of her other two grandchildren.

'You see, now we understand that life had moved on, but we had stayed the same,' Assunta explained. 'We brought up Lucia as we were brought up and expected her to be identical, but the world outside our walls was a different and more modern one and we ignored that influence.'

'You threw her out when she was pregnant,' Maya could not help reminding the older couple.

'We wanted her to agree to have the baby privately adopted, and she wouldn't.'

Maya sighed. 'Thank goodness she didn't or Izzy and I might never have known our parents.'

'I didn't think your father was good enough for her,' her grandfather admitted reluctantly. 'He was penniless and my daughter had never worked a day in her life.'

'They've had their problems with money management,' Maya confided wryly. 'But they are still very much in love with each other.'

Her grandparents looked relieved to hear that news, as if even though that marriage might not have been what they had wanted for their daughter, they were still pleased it had worked out for her.

Raffaele reappeared. 'Sorry to break this

up but the bride has to start getting dressed,' he announced.

And her grandmother was up in a trice, keen to accompany Maya. Before Maya left the room, he signalled a maid to show the older woman upstairs and said levelly to Maya, 'Did I make the right choice in letting them come?'

Maya smiled brightly and nodded simultaneously. 'Yes, you did. It was a little embarrassing admitting to them that this is a secret wedding, but I encouraged them to consider contacting my mother and I passed over the phone number,' she confided in a rush. 'I think there will eventually be a reconciliation. Everybody seems to be in the right place now for that to happen.'

'And your family being happy makes you happy?' Raffaele queried in apparent surprise.

'Doesn't yours?'

'I don't have a family. My mother's dead, I *first* met my father when I was twenty-one and my acquaintance with Aldo only began last month,' he told her flatly.

'I didn't realise any of that,' Maya admitted, silenced by those admissions, striving to think of what her life might have been like without the background of support and love that she pretty much took for granted. 'You're very alone.'

Raffaele shrugged and frowned. 'I'm a loner by nature. It hasn't harmed me.'

Maya almost dared to differ with that sentiment because it explained a lot to her—his lack of emotional understanding, for a start. 'You did something kind for me. I didn't think you were capable of that,' she admitted frankly.

Raffaele inclined his arrogant dark head and one of the staff approached with a pile of gift-wrapped boxes. 'It's a wedding gift.'

Her brow furrowed. 'Who from?'

Raffaele tensed, outrageously long black lashes curling up with incredulity. 'From me.'

'Oh…'

'I decided that I didn't want you wearing my mother's jewellery.'

Her facial muscles tightened. 'That's perfectly understandable.'

'No, you're misunderstanding me…*again*,' Raffaele stressed. 'For me, there's nothing but bad memories attached to my mother's jewellery, and I've now arranged to have it auctioned off. These jewels are new, and for you to wear and *keep*.'

Bad memories? Curiosity assailed her, furthered by the haunting darkness of his gaze. But she was also disconcerted and embarrassed because it would never have occurred to her to buy anything for him even as a token wedding gift. Maya nodded jerkily. 'Thank you very much.'

Raffaele gazed down at her in mounting frustration, craving something he wanted from her, unable to label it, only able to recognise by his own dissatisfaction that he wasn't receiving it. 'It's no big deal. I've got money to burn,' he fielded drily.

'I'd better go and start getting dressed,' Maya muttered, backing slowly away, her eyes locked involuntarily to the liquid burning gold of his.

'All I can think about is *undressing* you,' Raffaele confided without even thinking about it, and then he watched her face freeze and shutter and knew it had been the wrong thing to say. But *why* was it the wrong thing? Once again, he felt at a tactical disadvantage, as if everyone else but him had the right script in Maya's radius. She wanted him. He could see that in her eyes, when she looked at him with need and desire. What could be wrong with expressing that? Was she really that shy?

And if she *was* shy, how did he handle that? Because vast as his experience was, he had never been with a shy woman.

A maid leading the way, Maya hurried upstairs to arrive breathless in an opulent bedroom suite embellished with superb polished antique furniture. There a hair stylist, a make-up artist and her grandmother eagerly awaited the bride's arrival. Her *nonna* addressed the maid in Italian, ordering some drink that Maya had never heard of.

'We drink it at weddings,' Assunta Parisi assured her, her likeness to Maya's mother, Lucia, in her greying dark hair and warm eyes lifting Maya's spirits. 'It's wonderful that you speak Italian. Raffaele didn't mention that.'

'He doesn't know yet. He speaks to me in English. I picked it up from Mum when I was a child and then added Italian in as an additional course at university,' Maya admitted, and when the maid arrived with an elaborate decanter and fancy glasses, she felt that it would have seemed churlish for her to declare then that she didn't usually drink.

Anyway, she thought rebelliously as the preparation of the bride began, perhaps she needed a little pick-me-up to face what lay ahead: sex with Raffaele. Of course, she could get through that as long as she didn't think about the logistics of having to strip off in front of him, open her body to a virtual stranger and act as if it were no big deal. Easy-peasy, she told herself firmly, no silly timid bride here, as she drank down the sweet liqueur. A little while later, a faint buzz hazed her thoughts and she began to feel a tad more relaxed. So, one or two drinks just to grease the wheels of her family-saving marriage and why not? After all, she probably wouldn't be drinking while she was trying to get pregnant, she reasoned ruefully.

She had set the gift boxes on the dressing table when she entered the room and while the stylist was doing her hair, her *nonna* asked what they were and, learning, urged her to open them immediately. With reluctance, because gifts struck her as inappropriate in her non-relationship with Raffaele, she opened the first and everyone present gasped. The opened boxes revealed a king's ransom in jewels, ranging from a superb tiara to a necklace that was a glittering waterfall of diamonds.

Her *nonna* squeezed her shoulder and leant down to whisper, 'He told your *nonno* and I that it was a marriage of business, but he *lied*. No man gives such magnificence in *those* circumstances,' she assured her grandchild with proud satisfaction. 'You are very beautiful and educated and he has fallen in love. Finally, the old bitterness between our families will be buried and forgotten.'

Maya might have been betrayed into laughing out loud at that fanciful conviction had not the maid brought out the wedding gown to display to them. Her breath caught in her throat because it was gorgeous and absolutely not what she had expected when Raffaele had done the choosing. She had been prepared for something tight, revealing and sexy such as he preferred, not a dream of a long dress with fine lace sleeves, a fitted bodice and layers and layers of silk in the skirt that glistened with handmade embroidery and shimmering crystals. The most daring aspect of the gown was the cutaway above the waist, which would bare a section of her back, so not very daring at all, not chosen for him, but chosen by him for *her*, which was another surprise.

And she didn't *like* Raffaele surprising her, especially not after she had believed she understood him to perfection and had set him in stone to play his role as the spoiled, selfish and dissolute bridegroom. As her grandmother enthused about the wedding gown, wild horses could not have dragged the truth out of Maya, that in fact Raffaele had chosen the dress, because suddenly she was ashamed of that truth, that she had agreed to their marriage but had nonetheless *refused* to play *her* role. Shame made her reach for her glass of liqueur again and sip in haste because the alcohol was blurring her dark thoughts. She, who prided herself on being kind, fair and reasonable, had been mean, angry and resentful of a choice *she* had made because she *could* have walked away from Raffaele's offer.

Her fingers curled on her grandfather's arm as he escorted her proudly down the aisle of the picturesque country church, which was festooned with flowers and crammed with smiling, staring guests. The wedding had never felt more real to Maya than it did at that moment as her gaze travelled anxiously to the male awaiting her at the altar. There he stood, Raffaele Manzini, the last man alive she had expected to try to turn their business marriage into a more normal one when she had made no effort whatsoever. And he *was* beautiful, tall and lithe and dark and sleek, for once formally clad in his wedding finery, a light grey morning suit teamed with a cravat, waistcoat and tailored dress pants.

Her throat tightened, butterflies buzzing like bees in her taut stomach, every inch of her reacting to his raw masculinity, and it was so completely, utterly unnerving to Maya, who felt so threatened by that instinctive response, that she hastily dropped her gaze again.

They knelt on velvet cushions and the priest performed the ceremony in both English and Italian, yet once again mutiny and a sense of wrong stirred within Maya, who had only ever expected to wed in all sincerity and love. Raffaele eased a slender platinum band onto her finger and tugged her round to face him as though he intended to kiss her while their guests swelled the church with song in celebration of their rites.

'You look divine…like a breathtakingly beautiful ice maiden,' he whispered, stunning dark tawny eyes locked to her flawless face with an intensity she could feel, and it only made her tremble.

'It's cool in here,' she deflected with a faint shake in her voice, turning her head away from him in denial that he could make her feel so unlike herself.

Maya had never allowed a man to affect her, had believed that that was her choice alone, and now she was discovering different and it scared her. She met Raffaele's eyes and her body lit up like the sunrise at dawn, sexual awareness flooding her in an unstoppable tide, heat and tension gripping her. It made her feel out of control for the first time ever and she hated that.

On the steps of the church he introduced her to his great-grandfather, Aldo, the man she knew she had to blame for masterminding her predicament, she conceded. Yet how could she bestow blame on anyone when her family was finally free of the debts that had stolen their happiness for so many years? Deciding that she could not, she met Aldo's shrewd dark eyes, set in his worn face, with a smile.

'That was generous of you,' Raffaele remarked in surprise as the nurse accompanying Aldo wheeled the elderly man away again.

'As you reminded me,' Maya murmured stiffly, 'I picked this option.'

'We will both adapt to this, to *us* as a couple,' Raffaele pronounced with assurance.

'That you want me as much as I want you gives us a solid foundation.'

'Your idea of a foundation and mine are as far apart as the polar ice caps,' Maya fielded tightly, wishing that she could deny what he said but remembering that kiss with an inner shudder, that kiss that had taught her that she was utterly naïve when it came to sensual temptation. But what was the point in beating herself up about it when she should be grateful for that attraction with a wedding night lying ahead of them?

Her stomach began churning again and the first thing she did when they arrived back at the house, where a reception was being staged, was reach for a glass of champagne being proffered by a uniformed waiter.

Why was she so nervous about sex? Was it only that she didn't love Raffaele? Was it that she knew the first time might very likely hurt to some degree? Or was it simply that Raffaele was *already* making her feel far more than she was comfortable feeling for him? Her emotions were getting involved: he fascinated her.

The truth of that admission slivered through her like a threat because his attraction for her wasn't solely physical. No, the source of that deeper attraction lay in the seeming conflicts she sensed within him. On the surface, Raffaele was cool, logical and ruthless but deep down, where it didn't show to the outside world, Raffaele was actually intense and volatile and highly intelligent, capable of being unexpectedly sensitive to her wants and needs.

That was the man who had searched out her dream wedding gown and who had invited her long-lost Italian grandparents to attend their wedding to foster a family reunion for her benefit. There had also been the jewellery he had given her to replace items he had admitted would only resurrect bad memories for him. All those actions were very personal and specific and the very opposite of what she had expected from him.

'I thought you didn't touch alcohol,' Raffaele commented.

'A wedding should be an exception to any rule like that,' Maya fibbed, determined not to admit that she was so feeble that the alcohol was easing her nervous tension and relaxing her. Dutch courage, she had heard it called—well, today she needed it, lest somewhere in her mind she found that dangerous sexual attraction combining with deeper feelings of a more personalised nature. No, she wasn't foolish enough to make that mistake with the bridegroom.

She had noticed the effect Raffaele had on women, even in the church. Eyes trailing acquisitively over him and lingering before looking enviously at her, a feminine hunger that she recognised now that she had experienced it for herself. But Raffaele wasn't hers and never would be. He wanted the right to buy a giant technology company and she, as well as the child she might conceive, were the price. And that was *all* he wanted. Maya wasn't going to be the idiot who forgot that salient fact for a second.

In the aftermath of the luxury buffet, Raffaele swept her out onto the dance floor and she thought once again about how shockingly fast her life had changed. She had married a man who owned a home large enough to provide a fancy pillared party room with a dance floor. How weird was that?

His hand splayed across her hip as he steered her round the floor and she could feel him, lean and powerful, fingers lifting to her spine to feather against bare skin that had never felt more naked. It was a revelation that that little keyhole of unadorned skin above her waist could be that sensitive and she shivered, still fighting that response to a man she barely knew.

Raffaele tensed as once again his bride moved out of contact. It was as if she didn't want him when he knew she did. That desire was there in her eyes whenever she looked at him. Why did she then back away? His hand lifted from her shoulder and his fingers splayed to lace into the wondrous fall of her pale fair hair, tipping her head back, lifting her face to his. He collided with distrustful green eyes fresh as ferns and before he had even thought about it he was crushing that ripe pink mouth under his, plundering it with raw fervour.

Maya reacted to the burn of his sensual mouth on hers, setting her on fire in places she didn't want to think about but, even so, she was achingly aware of the tautness of her nipples and the yawning ache between her slender thighs. Closing him out didn't work—he burned through her defences like a blowtorch, she conceded grudgingly. Embrace that, her brain urged her; *fight* it, her instincts protested.

'I want a drink,' she told him, angling her head back, stepping away.

'You're driving me crazy. Is that the point?' Raffaele pressed with a ragged edge to his dark deep accented drawl, dark caramel eyes shimmering like gold lighting the shadows.

Maya was feeling dizzy, hazy.

Raffaele stared down at her dilated pupils and murmured, 'I think a drink is the last thing you need. Time for us to leave.'

'Leave?' she exclaimed in astonishment.

'We're leaving on my yacht, *Manzini One.*'

Manzini One? Self-important, much? Her tummy shimmied at the prospect of the sea and she breathed in deep and slow. 'I feel dizzy.'

'Of course, you do. You're drunk,' Raffaele pronounced, suddenly cool and judgemental in tone.

'I'm *not*!' Maya protested fiercely.

And she was still arguing the toss all the way through the polite goodbyes to their guests and into the helicopter, when silence fell because it demanded too much effort to talk over the noise of the rotor blades and, besides, she was beginning to feel a little bit queasy.

Unasked, Raffaele scooped her out of the helicopter and carried her down a wooden dock in silence.

'What are you doing?' she demanded sharply.

'What I have to do,' Raffaele parried grimly.

Maya groaned. 'I didn't intend to drink so much.'

'It's our wedding night,' Raffaele reminded her unnecessarily. 'This is not a good start. But when you said you didn't drink, was that a warning that you *shouldn't* drink?'

'No, this is my very *first* time ever intoxicated,' Maya told him with precision. 'Take that as you will.'

'Not a compliment.'

'Wasn't intended to be.'

'Was the idea of sex with me *that* offensive?' Raffaele growled in apparent disbelief.

'I know that you want me to say that it wasn't but the way I think, it would be wrong,' she framed apologetically.

'You're my bride! This is our wedding night,' Raffaele countered with startling ferocity.

'But you feel like a stranger,' his bride admitted in colloquial Italian before she passed out.

CHAPTER FIVE

MAYA WAKENED WITH a groan, tormented by the waking nightmare of the night she had passed.

Dawn light illuminated surroundings that were still only vaguely familiar. A big room, a glimpse of the sea through a window, a slight rolling gait in tune with the swell of the sea something else to be regretted alongside the amount of alcohol she had imbibed the day before. She scrambled out of bed, her head aching and still swimming, shame almost choking her. But the mortification of her splintered shards of memory was indescribably worse...

She recalled floundering like a landed fish on top of a pale marble floor and wanting to die, literally *die*. Worst of all, she recalled throwing up in that bathroom with Raffaele tugging her hair out of the way. She recalled Raffaele tucking her into bed, trying to get tea down her, failing because her stomach wasn't up to anything but water and even drinking that had been a challenge, she remembered with a shudder. Raffaele had looked after her; she remembered in shock that he had bothered, that he hadn't just stuck her in a yacht cabin to be sick without him as an audience. What did it say about her that she dearly wished he had simply abandoned her to her sufferings?

Sal was out on deck at dawn having a cigarette when Raffaele emerged from the couple of hours of sleep he had snatched and stepped onto the terrace with a cup of black coffee in his hand.

'So?' Sal challenged, smooth as glass. 'Marriage not quite what you expected?'

Raffaele breathed in deep and slow and strove to resist rising to the bait, but the temptation was too great. 'I thought she had more sense.'

'You blackmailed her… I can't imagine why she would be so sensitive,' Sal murmured softly.

Raffaele clenched his teeth together and said nothing at all, waiting until the older man went back inside before making the same move.

Maya emerged from the bathroom, every inch of her washed and shampooed and freshened, her slender body clad in denim shorts and tee shirt, but nothing could take the awful memories away. Her head was still sore. She winced as the cabin door opened. Cabin, she repeated ruefully to herself, for such an ordinary word in no way described the shining expanse of the wooden floor, the opulent upholstery, the glorious built-in furniture or the patio doors that led out onto a private terrace that was also splendidly equipped. When she glanced up to see who had entered and saw Raffaele carrying a tray, her knees gave way and she dropped down on the side of the bed sooner than look him in the eye.

'Feeling pretty rough?' Raffaele murmured flatly.

'Let's be frank… I deserve it,' Maya muttered. 'I can only say sorry—there's not much else I can say.'

Raffaele extended a glass of water to her. 'Painkillers,' he proffered, dropping a couple on her lap. 'No need to suffer if you don't need to.'

Maya snatched in a steadying breath and

took the pills, imbibing the water slowly, still terrified that she would start feeling ill again. Mercifully that phase of her recovery seemed to be over. 'I don't usually do stuff like this,' she sighed.

A table settled in front of her and a tray appeared on it. 'Eat.'

'I'm not hungry.'

'The food will help. *Eat,*' Raffaele repeated insistently. 'You speak Italian,' he added, switching languages. 'You didn't mention it.'

'It didn't seem important. You're happy speaking English.'

'But more at home with Spanish or Italian,' Raffaele told her gently.

Maya buttered a piece of toast and ate the egg on offer. She poured the tea, passing him a cup and saucer as he crouched down in front of her, cruelly enforcing eye contact.

And it *was* cruel, she reflected numbly, because in the daylight flooding through the windows they were wickedly beautiful eyes the colour of caramel or melted honey.

'If that wasn't the norm for you, I need to know why,' Raffaele murmured almost softly, as though he was trying to be persuasive or, at the very least, non-threatening.

Maya swallowed her tea. 'It's just the whole

situation,' she mused ruefully. 'I let it get to me. I won't let that happen again.'

'You didn't want to share a bed with me last night… I assume,' Raffaele continued lazily. 'Yet I believed you were attracted to me.'

Maya could feel her face starting to blossom in a dreadful slow-burning blush. 'I was…er… I am,' she admitted tightly, feeling that he deserved that much truth from her.

'So, what was the problem?' Raffaele enquired levelly as he set the tea down that she had handed him untouched.

Maya sipped her tea and stared down into it as if it might provide her with a miraculous rescue from the dialogue. 'I'm not very experienced.'

'Not a problem for me.'

'Actually, not experienced at all,' Maya confided thinly, resenting the need to invade her own privacy, but still feeling that she owed him an explanation for her less than adult behaviour.

Without warning, Raffaele vaulted upright again and moved out of view, utterly astonished by her admission but trying to hide the fact from her. 'Again,' he breathed a little gruffly, 'not a problem… I assume.'

'You…*assume*?' Maya prompted in surprise, glancing across the cabin at him, studying his long, straight, shirt-clad back as he gazed out through the sliding doors onto the terrace.

Raffaele swung fluidly around, dark deep-set eyes settling on her with sudden intensity. 'I'd be a liar if I told you I'd been a woman's first before. I think that the more honest we are with each other, the easier this marriage will be for both of us.'

'I agree with that,' Maya framed round an enormous yawn, her virtually sleepless night catching up with her even as much of her earlier awkwardness with him drained away and somehow without her noticing. 'But, you know, I'm not a child. I wasn't freaking out about the sex as much as…as…what are you doing?' she gasped.

Seeing that yawn, Raffaele had begun moving towards her even while she was speaking and, removing the cup from her hand, he set it down and bent to lift her off the side of the bed and then immediately lower her back down with her head on the pillows. 'You need more sleep,' he told her. 'I'm shattered too.'

Maya watched him toe off his canvas shoes and throw himself down on the other side of the bed with wide anxious eyes.

'I didn't get much sleep last night either,' Raffaele pointed out. 'I'll keep my clothes on though, since I suppose anything else would freak you out.'

'Oh, don't be silly,' Maya mumbled, her face reddening. 'I don't mind if you get undressed.'

He unbuttoned his shirt and sighed, stretching out his long, lean, powerful frame. 'I don't think I can be bothered.'

Maya lifted her head and looked down at him, the curling black lashes resting on his high cheekbones in a flawless masculine face. The shirt lay open now, revealing a long bronzed slice of muscular torso. 'Take the shirt and the jeans off or you'll be uncomfortable,' she instructed drily.

Raffaele's eyes flew open again and a sudden grin slashed his wide perfect mouth and stole away the darkness that often edged his strong features. 'Only if you have the guts to match me.'

Impatience gripping her, Maya peeled off her tee and wriggled free of her shorts, pushing them off the bed. She had forgotten that she wasn't wearing a bra and, flustered by the knowledge that she had bared her breasts for his benefit, she wrenched the sheet back on the bed and scrambled beneath it to close her eyes, acknowledging that she truly felt as if she could sleep for a week.

For a split second as he took in that view of her pale pert breasts, Raffaele had frozen halfway out of his shirt but, gritting his teeth, he shed the shirt in a heap and embarked on his jeans.

'I'm afraid I'm going commando,' he warned her.

'I'm not looking…couldn't care less.'

'Maybe I want you to *want* to look—maybe my male ego is squashed by this amount of disinterest,' Raffaele murmured with sibilant bite.

'A twenty-ton weight couldn't squash your ego,' Maya mumbled soothingly, sliding a hand below a pillow and tucking her cheek gratefully into its soft support because he was correct: she had never felt so tired in her life. It was as if all the stresses, all the fears and worries that had dogged her over the past weeks had all homed in on her at once and she was exhausted, mentally and physically.

'You're doing a very good job all on your own.' Raffaele listened to the soft sound of her breathing ease into a regular rhythm while tension kept his own tiredness at bay.

When had he last been with a woman who

didn't *want* anything from him? He couldn't remember. It had started so far back in his life with his mother's incomprehensible demands. If it wasn't attention a woman wanted from him, it was sex or money or the desire to show him off like a trophy in public. That knowledge had forged an iron barrier inside Raffaele and for the first time Maya was making him realise that it wasn't that he was unfeeling, it wasn't that he didn't have emotions, it was that he had walled them up behind that barrier. Every time he had seen someone reveal humanity's worst traits of cruelty and greed, he had felt justified in his outlook, and it had never occurred to him until that moment that he would one day be cruel and greedy too and visit those ugly qualities on the woman he had trapped into marrying him.

No, he *hadn't* blackmailed her, he *hadn't* forced her in any way, he rationalised with confidence. Facts were facts: Maya had made her own choice when she decided to save her parents from their mistakes and had paid with her freedom. But it was also fact that he didn't *need* the Parisi technology company to survive and that he had pushed her into their current predicament simply because he was bored and in search of a fresh business challenge. He wasn't, he decided, a good enough person to decide that he regretted what he had done: *he didn't*. But he was also burning to possess Maya with a hunger that was deeply unfamiliar to him, in spite of his rich, varied past experience of women.

Because she was a challenge? Because she didn't seem to want him as much as he wanted her to want him? Was he really that shallow, that arrogant?

Or was it because she had some strange unidentifiable quality that revved his libido? Was sex really that important to him? He would've claimed it wasn't. After all, it had been weeks since he had last had sex, because sex had become as lacklustre as everything else in his life. At least, he could be grateful to Maya for returning him to the sexual land of the living, he conceded grimly, amused by the tent in the sheet over his hips. His handsome mouth quirked as she burrowed her hips into his thigh with a sleepy murmur. With care, he gently pushed her back from him because he didn't need the temptation and he didn't do affection. Loving or even highly valuing anyone or anything in his life was too risky, too dangerous, as he had learned at a very early age.

* * *

Maya wakened slowly to a room that had been plunged into the warm peach and golden shadows of the afternoon. Checking her watch, she saw that she had slept several hours away and she was about to sit up when the bathroom door opened and Raffaele stalked out stark naked, a towel still in one hand as he dried his wet black hair, leaving it tousled and damp and spiky.

Clothed, Raffaele was intimidating, naked he was even more magnificently overwhelming. He had the physique of a Greek God, carved in vibrant warm bronzed flesh rather than cold marble. From his broad shoulders to his powerful torso, narrow hips and long, strong legs, he was a vision of sleek masculine virility such as she had never seen in real life. Her bemused attention roamed down over the hard contours of his muscular chest to the corrugated lean flatness of his stomach, lingering on the silky line of dark hair that furrowed down over his belly…and there her gaze froze, wide with dismay.

'Well, don't look at me like that if you don't want *that* to happen.' Raffaele laughed with rich appreciation as she reddened and turned her head away. 'You can't be that innocent.'

'I was more into mathematics than men,' Maya fielded as Raffaele, still gloriously, unashamedly naked, came down on the bed beside her and left her breathless.

He lifted a dark brow and frowned, as if he could not comprehend that amount of indifference. 'Always?'

Maya shrugged a bare shoulder. 'It's just the way I'm wired.'

'It's insidiously attractive…'

Maya looked up into brilliant dark eyes that had the glitter of stars below his curling lashes and her heart jumped beneath her ribs and began a slow heavy pound, her body in a sort of heavy stasis that seemed to have nothing to do with her brain. He lifted a hand slowly, brown fingers curving to her cheekbone, and those stunning eyes of his, as dark and riveting as polished jet, held hers, heat pulsing through her in an involuntary rush, the sheer basic attraction that had freaked her out the day before flowing through her, and suddenly she was questioning why she was fighting what she was feeling because he no longer felt like a stranger.

He had reunited her with her grandparents, given her fabulous jewellery and looked after her when she was drunk in a way she would never have expected him to do. Underneath that façade of his, he was not inherently cruel, not innately cold, he was a much more enthralling mix.

'...ensuring that I have the greatest difficulty keeping my hands off you,' he confided in hoarsened completion.

And it was as if something simply snapped into place inside Maya and she stretched up a couple of inches to lay her lips against his as she urged, 'Don't—'

'Maya?'

'Less talk, more action,' she muttered boldly, letting the desire and the fascination take charge of her for the first time ever.

And finally, he kissed her, and it was as if her body had been waiting all her life for that sweet wildness to engulf her from her head to her toes, leaving her feeling almost detached from the self she had thought she knew. She moved to sit up, but his hand splayed across her spine, pushing her back against the pillows, controlling the pace with a masculine urgency that she found indescribably sexy. His lips parted hers and his tongue delved deep and tangled with her own, sending a tide of electrifying hunger pulsing through her with the efficacy of a drug in her bloodstream.

That fast, she discovered that she wanted more, was indeed impossibly greedy for more of him, and it shocked her to recognise that deep-down craving she had fought to restrain as though it were toxic when, indeed, it seemed to be exactly what she needed most. As Raffaele lowered his mouth to the straining pout of her rosy nipples and lingered there, toying with the stiff crests, her heartbeat hammered like crazy and a wash of heat engulfed her pelvis. It occurred to her that, only hours earlier, she had been ducking behind a sheet, pretty much embarrassed to show off that part of her because she didn't have very much to offer in the boob department, as he himself had once noted.

'I like…' Raffaele told her with a brazen smile that was very Manzini, framing the small mounds in splayed fingers, a thumb caressing each throbbing tip. 'Just enough, not too much and real.'

'Hope you can say the same about your own anatomy,' Maya quipped, shocked at herself for that response and staring at him with shaken eyes, thinking, I did not say that, that is not me.

Raffaele burst out laughing and gazed down at her with startled dark golden eyes.

'You give as good as you get…right? That's good. It's a quality you need with me, *bellezza mia*,' he told her with surprising sincerity. 'I can be—'

'Challenging?' Maya slotted in helplessly. 'I noticed.'

Raffaele grinned and kissed her again, his hands roaming over a body that already felt fiercely sensitised to his touch. The throb pulsing at the apex of her thighs was new to her, making her shift restlessly, her hips rising with a hunger she only recognised subliminally because thought didn't seem possible in the midst of her growing physical excitement. The feather-soft touch of a finger just *there* and she could feel herself lighting up like a forest fire, nerve endings jumping, a mesmerising warmth enthralling her feminine core while the slick dampness gathered.

'It's like an equation. You and me and the parameters,' Maya pronounced with a glorious smile of discovery.

'OK,' Raffaele agreed, because he didn't know what she was talking about but it seemed to be making her happy.

'I bet I could make a model of it!' she exclaimed, her brain already homing in on the possibilities.

And Raffaele could see that she was ready to leap out of bed and look for a whiteboard or some such thing to engage in the kind of mathematics that inflamed her meteoric brain. 'But not right now,' he told her urgently. 'Right now, we stay on task.'

Maya blinked up at him, green eyes limpid as ferns with sheer disappointment, and he kissed her again because it felt like the only thing he could do to distract her. And it worked, mercifully it *worked*, he conceded, shaken up by that experience when he himself was utterly lost in the magic of her response to him.

'I'm burning up for you, *bellezza mia*,' he growled.

'Oh…' Maya trailed gentle fingers through his wildly tousled black hair. 'I've messed up your hair, clutching it.'

'Go right ahead,' he encouraged, dragging in a sustaining breath, his broad chest expanding that something about him could hold her interest.

'You don't mind?' That glorious smile was angled at him again.

Out of words, Raffaele crushed her mouth under his again, struggling to stay in control, fighting not to fall on her like an animal, a hunger of storm-force potency driving him. It was, without a doubt and yet utterly inexplicably to him, the most exciting sexual experience of his life.

'I want you too,' she whispered unevenly, her body quivering, shifting up to his in invitation as the unbearable longing stabbed at her afresh.

He slid over her, easing into her, giving her time to adjust to that unfamiliar intrusion. Maya tried not to tense and looked up into his taut, intent face, the lustrous dark eyes alight with a hunger as deep as her own. Something she hadn't even known she was worrying about quieted within her because she saw that he was fighting for control as much as she was. There was a momentary sharp piercing pain and then that introduction was over and there was only the rousing stimulation of feeling her own body stretch to accept the fullness of his. From the first subtle shift of his hips, she was needy, wanting, aglow with the discovery of that enthralling newness.

Fierce sensation assailed her, and her eyes widened, the spark of excitement flashing into a flame that burned in the most pleasurable of ways. More, she wanted to shout, *more*, and it took effort to stay silent while the raw excitement roaring through her built and built until finally he was slamming into her, wonderfully wild and passionate, and she was urging him on with her body in the only way she knew how, legs wrapping round him, nails turned into talons raking down his smooth spine in her insistence.

She soared to a peak that sent her flying into a million pieces, her whole body consumed by that intensity that lifted her to an unimaginable high and then left her floating in a sea of drowning pleasure.

'That was amazing,' Maya sighed. 'Thank you.'

And that quickly, Raffaele knew what it was about Maya that intrigued him. He had never met a woman like her, never had sex with a woman like her, never even dreamt that a woman like her even existed because she was *so* different that she smashed every one of his trite expectations.

'That was my line,' Raffaele husked in an informative tone as he lifted his head from the tumbled swathes of her blonde hair, which smelled like strawberries, he noted abstractedly as he levered his weight off her and slid to one side.

'No, that's basic relationship stuff,' Maya informed him with superiority. 'If you do something well, I should praise you for it.'

'Like you're training a pet?' Raffaele derided.

'Well, if you're going to take offence at the most innocent comment,' Maya countered.

'Allow me to warn you…tact is not your biggest strength,' Raffaele pointed out with another grin.

'Oh, I know that,' Maya replied without concern. 'You're not the first person to label me socially awkward. I live inside my head most of the time. I'm not observant either.'

In wonderment, Raffaele watched her slide out of the bed and away from him, no hanging around, no after-sex fondling, cuddling, absolutely nothing sought from him. 'Where are you going?' he asked lazily.

'I need a shower. Sex is messy,' Maya sighed.

Raffaele raised an ebony brow. 'I think you're supposed to lie flat for a while afterwards if you're trying to get pregnant,' he murmured silkily.

Maya blinked and walked back to the bed like a naked forest nymph with her hair flowing round her. Beneath his arrested gaze, she lay down again. Felled by an old wives' tale, he conceded in fascination, but for some strange reason he didn't want her washing him off her again and walking away from him.

'How long do I have to lie here for?'

'Ten minutes should be enough,' Raffaele breathed, trying very hard not to laugh because she looked as trapped as he had often felt when women tried to hold *him* by their side and that was a novel experience, not entirely to his satisfaction. He would, he appreciated, have to learn how to cuddle if he wanted her to stay with him afterwards. And *why* would he want that?

'This is *so*…do you have a pen and paper?' Maya asked suddenly, wondering if she could come up with an equation that matched them as a couple and their relationship and calculating the probabilities.

Raffaele reached over and provided her with both from the nightstand nearest him. He lay back watching as she covered line after line with what to him were incomprehensible mathematical notations. Every so often she paused, smooth brow furrowing while she pondered, and then she would be off onto a fresh page, so wrapped in her calculations that he reckoned that a volcanic eruption would not have penetrated her concentration.

He went for a shower and when he emerged, she was still at it and she hadn't glanced up once. It was as if he had vanished; it was as if he didn't exist. He discovered that he absolutely loathed that sensation. It reminded him of the frequent occasions when his mother had forgotten his needs as a child, overlooking the necessity of his eating or sleeping. Of course, his mother, Julieta, had often lived in her own world, cocooned from reality.

'We're getting off the boat,' he told her loudly.

A thousand miles away, for all he knew mentally on another planet, she looked up at him, beautiful sea-glass eyes distant.

'We've arrived at the island where we're spending our honeymoon,' Raffaele extended.

'Oh...' Maya gasped, blinking to take in the sea of paper surrounding her and her still naked, unwashed state. 'I zoned out, didn't I?'

'You did,' Raffaele agreed.

'Don't dump anything!' she warned him as she leapt off the bed and vanished into the bathroom.

Raffaele picked an outfit out of the new

wardrobe she had yet to discover, gossamer-fine undies in lilac, a strappy sundress. He knocked on the bathroom door and entered when she shouted out, *'Yes?'* sounding very harassed.

'Clothes,' Raffaele announced, resting them down on a chair, thinking for a second and then yanking out towels for her use as well because he wasn't sure she would find them on her own. He had never had to look after anyone or anything in many, many years and it felt weird.

'Marriage not quite what you expected?' Sal had mocked. Raffaele conceded that at least he wasn't bored.

'Oh, that was kind of you,' Maya remarked, swathing herself in a towel. 'That's what Izzy does when she's trying to hurry me up...my goodness, those aren't *my* clothes—'

'They are now. I bought them for you.'

Maya sent him a glance that suggested that he was in some way strange and sort of shrugged, not interested enough in clothes, it seemed, to enquire any further. Raffaele stepped back out again and within minutes she emerged, none of the lengthy feminine preparation for his company that he was used to receiving apparent in her appearance. She had combed her wet hair, hadn't bothered to dry it, only braid it, and yet *still* she drew his gaze like a magnet. Something about that slender, leggy, graceful figure, those delicate features or that unexpectedly luscious pink mouth exuded radical appeal.

Maya focused on Raffaele, a sort of creeping shyness briefly enfolding her as she allowed herself to finally recall that experience in the bed with him. Transcendent, earth-shattering, she mused with a little inner quiver she could not suppress. She had never dreamt that sex might be addictive like that. Was it only because she had been with *him*? Or was something deeper involved? Was she starting to feel more than she should for him? Surely not? She was not stupid. And yet the pull he exerted over her was extreme, her eyes constantly needing to stray back to him.

That seemed to be what that physical chemistry could deliver, and she should accept a blessing where she could find one in their business marriage, she told herself urgently. At least, trying to get pregnant wasn't going to be a disgusting ordeal. She really should only deal with Raffaele with logic. All the emotion she was fighting around him could be a disaster in the making, she reasoned worriedly, terrified of getting attached to him in any way. She wouldn't *allow* herself to feel anything for him and that would keep her safe from hurt or disillusionment.

The launch carved a sure passage through the deep blue Mediterranean Sea to the small island that lay ahead. It was an exhilarating ride and all Maya could see of the island was a pale sand beach fringed by trees with a glimpse of a low roof somewhere behind them. Honeymoon, she mused uneasily—it hadn't occurred to her that he would take such a conventional path to his objective.

Raffaele gazed stonily ahead, refusing to acknowledge the nightmare glimmers of his memories. He wasn't a sensitive guy, he didn't look back to the past and dwell unhealthily on it, no, he put it behind him, which was why he had chosen to bring Maya there to this superficially very beautiful little islet, which was both convenient and suitable for purpose.

Even so, when he swept a laughing Maya up into his arms and brought her down on the soft pale sand he had often played on as a child, his stomach still churned sickly when he too stepped out of the launch.

'The path's up here,' he murmured, moving ahead of her as guide, refusing to surrender to that queasiness in his gut because only the frightened, traumatised child he had once been would react that way.

'You've been here before?'

'It's one of my late mother's many properties, like the villa where we held the wedding. I used the villa because Aldo isn't able to travel far now and I'm using Aoussa—as it's called—because…because it makes sense to use it.'

As they walked beneath the palm trees lining the walkway, something in that uncharacteristic hesitation in his dark deep drawl furrowed her brow and filled her with a sense of unease. 'Did you grow up here?'

'No, Julieta used it for summer breaks or simply when she was in the mood to be alone…aside of the staff,' he told her curtly. 'She brought all her new husbands here, her lovers. Aoussa was one of her favourite places.'

'Did you lose your mother recently?' Maya prompted, seeking an explanation for the tension he couldn't hide. It was etched in the taut lines and hollows forming across his strong bone structure.

'Julieta has been gone ten years. I was in

my final year at boarding school when she died.' Raffaele strode on, determined to overcome the reactions assailing him because he was not weak or vulnerable any longer, he was a man, a *strong* man.

'You didn't call her Mother?'

'No. She didn't like to be called that,' Raffaele admitted gruffly.

An unexpectedly large building lay beyond the trees. It was all on one level, probably ultra-modern in its day with its many windows looking out over the ornamental gardens or towards the sea and shore exposed on the other side of the island. 'It is beautiful and clearly well maintained,' Maya commented. 'How long is it since your last visit?'

Raffaele thrust open the front door. 'Twenty-odd years,' he admitted grudgingly. 'Julieta went off it.'

In silence, Maya raised a brow, walking off on her own through big airy rooms, furnished in timeless style. She couldn't even begin to imagine owning a house that she hadn't visited in two decades or the level of wealth that could allow such lavish behaviour. She peered out into an interior courtyard and opened the door, turning her head to see where Raffaele was and immediately realising that something was wrong.

He was poised by the full-length windows staring out into the courtyard, his lean hands coiled into fists and trembling by his side, a sheen of perspiration gleaming on his bronzed face. Every muscle in his body was rigid.

'Raffaele…?' she began uncertainly.

'I'm not sure I *can* stay here,' he muttered raggedly, lifting a shaking hand to rake it through his luxuriant black hair. 'I had a flashback. I haven't had one in many years. It happened out there before breakfast.'

Compassion stirred in Maya; her gentle heart touched because that Raffaele could be vulnerable in his own hidden way had not once occurred to her. Instantly she was dismayed by the one-dimensional view she had taken of him. 'A flashback of what?' she pressed, moving across to him, one slender hand closing over one of his, her arm curving round the base of his spine in an effort to urge him towards the seating area to the left of them.

'Of Julieta killing my dogs,' he mumbled sickly.

CHAPTER SIX

REELING WITH SHOCK at that revelation as they sank down, Maya looked up into haunted dark golden eyes and her heart clenched as though someone had squeezed it. 'Why on earth would your mother have done something so dreadful?'

And he told her about Julieta then, and the day she had pulled out a gun over breakfast while he was playing with his childhood pets, how she had accused him of loving the dogs more than he loved her. In her adolescence, his mother had suffered a serious head injury and brain damage in a car accident, and it was after the crash that her mental health issues had developed. Although she had received many different diagnoses and had endured an ever-changing regime of medication, no treatment and no therapy had ever given her peace or normality.

'She can't be held responsible for anything wrong that she did. She was rarely in rational control of herself,' Raffaele pointed out with creditable loyalty. 'Unfortunately for me, her wealth and her lawyers protected her from outside interference.'

'You were eight years old, Raffaele. *Who* was looking after you?'

'The domestic staff generally took care of my physical needs, but they couldn't protect me from her because she sacked them immediately if they tried to intervene,' Raffaele admitted curtly.

'And your father?'

'Julieta shut Tommaso out of our lives while I was still a baby,' he explained. 'They were only married for a couple of years. He offended my mother by trying to compensate some waitress she had had fired in a restaurant and she threw him out. He had been cast off by the Manzinis when he married her and, in the divorce, he didn't get anything because their marriage hadn't lasted long enough. He didn't have the money to fight her through the courts for access to his son. He didn't have any choice in what followed.'

'So, tell me about the dogs,' she encouraged softly, reaching out to link her fingers carefully with his taut ones, noticing how he glanced down at their entangled hands with bemused discomfiture as they sat side by side on the sofa. 'And stop beating yourself up for being human, Raffaele. You went through an appalling experience as a child. It's still totally masculine *and* normal to be upset by the memory of it.'

Faint colour flared over his exotic cheekbones at that assurance but he let it go past. 'Bella and Lupo were puppies when they arrived that summer. I adored them,' he declared simply. 'They were the closest thing to a family that I ever had. They loved me back.'

'Didn't your mother love you?'

'If she did, she wasn't capable of showing it. She was very possessive of me, though. Nannies weren't allowed to show me physical affection, even if I was hurt or ill. With Julieta,' Raffaele revealed absently with a lack of emotion that cut Maya deep, 'it was half beating me to death one week and then a trip to Disneyland with every conceivable extra the next, all extremes, while she flailed from one mood into another.'

'There was physical abuse?' Maya queried with a concealed shudder and only belatedly did she recall him saying, when she had tried to slap him in his office, 'Nobody hits me now.'

'She was subject to uncontrollable rages. I was the most convenient target. Staff just quit on the spot if she lost her head with them.' Raffaele's fingers tensed in hers. 'I have scars all down my back from the time she took a belt to me. There was nobody to stop her except the nanny and Sal, who was a new employee. The nanny waited until the last possible moment to shout for Sal and I almost died from blood loss and shock. It was all hushed up, of course, by her lawyers. Julieta tried to sack Sal afterwards, but the lawyers insisted that he remain to look after my welfare. Julieta hated him but she couldn't get rid of him and there were no more beatings. If only Sal had been around when my dogs were alive, he would have got the gun off her. The night I first met Aldo, he admitted that he'd heard a rumour about my mistreatment around that time and that he'd tried to visit me. But Julieta wouldn't consent to him seeing me.'

Maya sat listening in a growing pool of horror. She had assumed that he had had it so easy all his life...*all that money*. But instead, he had lived a nightmare, rich but unloved, neglected while being both over-indulged and abused. All of a sudden she understood so much more about Raffaele Manzini from his apparent lack of emotion to his granite cool. It was *all* a front, there to convince every-body, not least him, that he had survived and flourished despite his appalling childhood.

'What age were you then?' she whispered.

'At the time of the beating? Maybe nine... I only remember fragments of it,' he mut-tered uncomfortably. 'Let's not dwell on this, Maya. It happened, it's done, it's over.'

'But you're still feeling it, you're still liv-ing it,' she told him gently.

'I don't want to,' he breathed in a raw bit-ter undertone. 'I don't want to *feel* anything!'

'I know...well...er... I can imagine,' she whispered ruefully, overwhelmed by her new awareness of the inner self he had success-fully concealed from her. She also knew that she would never again feel short-changed for her childhood with parents who were hopeless with money but who had absolutely adored their children and treated them accordingly.

Raffaele snatched in a steadying breath and his ebony brows pleated. 'How did you get all that out of me?' he demanded abruptly. 'I've never talked about it before.'

'I got you at a weak moment. Don't feel bad—we all have them and sometimes it's good for you to talk,' she soothed, looking up into eyes that were pure golden enticement in the sunlight, inky dark lashes enhancing them.

And the silence smouldered.

Raffaele's grip on her hand tightened and he reached down with his other hand to curve it to her hip and lift her up easily onto his lap. 'I want you,' he told her boldly.

Maya rolled her eyes at him. 'That's only because you feel ill at ease after telling me all that private stuff. It's a natural reaction for a macho male personality. You're trying to compensate.'

'No, it's a natural reaction to being with a very beautiful, compassionate woman, who also happens to be my wife,' Raffaele corrected in a driven undertone. '*I...want...you.* Right here, right now.'

Maya released a long-suffering sigh because he was so irredeemably *basic*, in no way adjusted to his own emotional prompts and what drove him at any given moment. 'Raffaele,' she began.

A split second after she parted her lips, he forced them apart with the delving lick of his tongue and she gasped. Logic became too steep a hill to climb as the burn of the hunger he could induce in her without effort began to infiltrate her quivering body. Beneath her she could feel him hard and ready, the jeans he sported doing nothing to conceal his arousal, and she felt a piercing pulse of hunger kick up between her thighs even though she still ached there from their earlier encounter. Once again, it rewrote all her assumptions that once that desire was sated, it would stay quiet for a good while and wouldn't unduly bother her again. All of a sudden she was hot, needy and desperate and twisting on his lap, grinding down on him with ridiculous enthusiasm, making him laugh, rough and low in this throat in that infuriating way of his, as if he knew some things better than she did, which, she finally conceded, he possibly did...

What followed was wild and passionate in a way she had never envisaged herself being. He hauled her up into his arms and carried her into a bedroom with a ridiculously huge bed surrounded by mirrored furniture that threw up far too many disorientating reflections.

'Yuck,' she commented on the décor.

'*Si*, I should've organised a refurbishment,'

Raffaele muttered in exasperation as he, very briefly, took the opportunity to look around himself and then froze.

Just taking in his pallor, Maya registered that memories had stolen him away from her again and she yanked him down shamelessly on the silly giant bed, slender hands smoothing up over long muscular thighs to gently brush the revealing bulge at his pelvis and, that fast, Raffaele was back in tune with her again, rolling her over on the bed and kissing her breathless. He was frantic for her, which she perfectly understood after the secrets he had shared and the effect on him of having to relive them. What she did *not* understand was that she should be equally frantic for him. After all, nothing distressing had happened to her. She had merely been an observer, an available listener, yet everything he had confided had somehow touched her too and his pain had distressed her.

When Raffaele flipped her over onto her knees and drove into her with urgent force, that scorching passion was somehow what she expected from him in that moment. She was not surprised or shocked or even standing outside herself marvelling because he had already taught her to expect that wild incredible flood of excitement. The sheer physical release of sex was a necessity for Raffaele after those confessions about his unhappy past. He couldn't handle the emotions, but he could vent them the only way he knew how. His hunger, his sudden overpowering need for her, was as much an expression of distress as he was capable of making and it both saddened and delighted her that he had turned to her for comfort. Yet that intense sharing of his had released something in her as well, she acknowledged, and made her feel much closer to him.

'So...' Maya refused to let go of him in the aftermath because even if he didn't know it, she *knew* he needed to be held. Her fingers smoothed down his long spine, feeling the slight roughness of scarring there, remembering what he had told her about that beating his mother had inflicted on him. Her eyes prickled and she stroked a soothing hand over his back, wishing fiercely that she could take the pain of that recollection from him, that knowledge that the person who should have most protected him had damaged him instead. He was still struggling to catch his breath and her body was humming with an unbelievable surfeit of pleasure and she pressed her mouth softly across his shoulder in an affectionate caress she could not withhold. 'Obviously you're not still planning to stay here in this house.'

'Why not?'

'Since it's clear that this is not a happy place for you,' Maya retorted bluntly. 'And what would we do here anyway?'

Raffaele studied her with glittering wicked eyes. 'What we're doing now.'

Maya rolled her eyes.

Raffaele laughed, relaxation winging through him. It was true: he hated the house but it had taken Maya to make him admit the fact. 'I'll visit the spot above the beach where the dogs were buried and then we'll get back on the yacht and tour with lots of sex included,' he compromised.

'Either you should sell this little island or demolish the house and rebuild,' Maya told him, ignoring the 'lots of sex' quip even though it irritated her. 'It shouldn't have been sitting here for so many years empty and unused.'

Raffaele released his breath on a slow hiss. 'I married an alpha woman, keen to remake me. Why didn't I spot the warning signs?'

Beneath his intent gaze, Maya scrunched

up her small nose. 'Because you were too full of yourself to believe that an alpha woman could talk common sense?'

Raffaele winced and then suddenly grinned. 'It's possible…but here you are.'

'Here I am,' Maya murmured, both arms wrapped round him as she surveyed him and the lustrous dark golden eyes locked to her like magnets.

And, he reflected, this kind of holding is fine and meaningless. He might not have enjoyed a relationship in which such affection existed before, but he trusted himself enough to believe that emotion didn't come into it for him. How could it possibly when he didn't feel what he was supposed to feel? He should never have brought her to the island, never have told her what had happened in the house, should never have dropped his guard to that extent. He had made three mistakes in succession, he conceded grimly. No good ever came from letting people get too close, he reminded himself stubbornly. Maya was hotter than hot in bed and, in addition to her intelligence, it was a winning combination for their marriage. In fact, he could not have done better, he mused, because she picked up on his moods as well as a weathervane forecasting a storm. But then, she was a clever woman, a very clever woman, and no doubt as detached as he was from anything deeper developing between them.

Maya drifted awake thinking about her sister, Izzy, and missing her. She was alone in bed and that was typical, because Raffaele always rose at the crack of dawn to spend a few hours working in his on-board office. Taking over his great-grandfather's business empire had kept him incredibly busy.

Just over a month had passed since the wedding and the secrecy Maya had embraced on that score had driven a wedge between her and the sister she loved, she conceded unhappily. Although they had talked with apparent openness on the phone during those weeks, Maya was stuck with the lie that she had taken a job in Italy. Yet how could she possibly tell Izzy the truth without upsetting her? Izzy, already dealing with an unplanned pregnancy and a new relationship in a foreign country, would be distraught if she knew what Maya had agreed to do to protect their parents and Matt.

Yet right now, there was a chance that Maya could be pregnant too and it was with a fierce desire to know, one way or another, that Maya slid out of bed. Her head swam dizzily as she straightened and moved into the bathroom to dig out one of the tests she had bought the day before and buried deep in the back of a cupboard. Her hands were a little unsteady as she sat down and unwrapped the box to pull out the instructions. The test was very simple, unlike her marriage, she conceded ruefully.

If she was pregnant, the marriage as such would be virtually over because that was what had been decided at the outset when she had insisted on exclusivity. Raffaele had agreed to stay faithful only until she conceived. He wanted his freedom back, the freedom to go out and sleep with other women. Why did the idea of that bother her? Why, when she had suspected for more than a week that she could have conceived, had she taken so long to buy the tests?

She had told Raffaele off for imagining he should be more than human that day on the island of Aoussa and now here she was being guilty of expecting more than she should from herself. After all, how could she live in such an intimate relationship with a man who attracted her and feel absolutely nothing for him? That wasn't realistic. At least not for her and her generous heart, it wasn't. Raffaele, though? Now that was a very different ball game.

Unlike her, Raffaele had spent a lifetime carefully ensuring that he felt very little for anyone. That was how he had got over his dysfunctional beginning in life; that was how he had learned to cope. Was he even capable of changing? And why would he even *want* to change when he was perfectly content as he was?

Yet that indifference in him to the more tender emotions scared and intimidated Maya, she acknowledged reluctantly. On his terms, she was just a business project and the child he wanted to conceive merely a useful tool that would give him the right to buy her grandfather's technology company. On her terms, however, Raffaele was the guy she had hated when she married him and then somehow, incomprehensibly to her, he had turned into a man she was learning to love…

How could she be falling for Raffaele Manzini? How could the impossible have happened? A sea change had taken place inside her that day on the island as soon as she understood what he had suffered because he had *shown* her his vulnerability. With that single act he had broken through her barriers and demolished her defences. She had stood above the beach with him where the dogs were buried and tears had misted her eyes when she'd seen the mound of pebbles he had gathered to mark the spot and the rough cross, cobbled together from driftwood by the gardener, Raffaele had explained. And, unfortunately for her, the way he had treated her since then had only encouraged the warmth of her developing feelings.

To date, being married to Raffaele was nothing at all as she had expected. He was wonderfully caring towards her and always coming up with new ways to please or entertain her. They had cruised the Mediterranean in the yacht, stopping off in random places to shop or explore ruins or sheltered coves and dine out, the very casualness of their itinerary relaxing.

And when it came to anything she might want, nothing was too much trouble for Raffaele. A reference to her interest in archaeology had led to a surprise flight to Egypt and the fulfilment of a lifelong dream to see the tombs in the Valley of the Kings. Raffaele wasn't into any of that and yet he had still patiently, considerately ensured that she also toured the treasures in the Cairo Museum, saw the pyramids and caught another flight to visit the temples at Luxor. He had devoted an entire energetic ten days to her enjoyment of antiquities. Her fingers toyed abstractedly with the gold sphinx necklace he had given her as a memento of their stay.

He had given her a feast of memories that she would remember all her life. He had even had a cabin on the yacht set up for her to work in, complete with whiteboards and cutting-edge technology. Even if she worked all day and late into the night, he didn't complain. No, he certainly wasn't clingy, but he was capable of interrupting her to remind her to eat or to initiate sex, she conceded with a rueful grin.

For over a month she had lived in a fantasy world with a gorgeous guy who behaved as if she was so incredibly beautiful and alluring that he couldn't resist her. Sexually, Raffaele was insatiable and yet the same man had admitted to her that prior to their wedding he hadn't sought the release of sex for weeks because he had become bored with it. Only he could scarcely afford to be bored with sex when his main goal was to conceive a child, she reminded herself sourly. And only an idiot like herself could have forgotten that reality for long enough to become infatuated with him. *I don't get attached to people*, he had warned her at the outset. With an angry snort at her own act of self-destruction, Maya finally stood up to check the test wand and see the result.

And there it was, exactly what she had expected: a positive.

Warm acceptance diametrically opposed to the furious self-loathing she had just been dealing with flooded Maya. No matter how she felt about Raffaele or her reactions to him, Maya wanted her baby and was excited at the prospect of becoming a mother. Yes, it was happening to her when she was younger than she had planned but Maya had always wanted children and could not be anything other than happy with such a result. Pausing only to brush her teeth and run a brush through her tumbled blonde hair, Maya walked back into the bedroom.

'Well?' Raffaele shot at her expectantly.

The sight of him when she was unprepared still left her short of breath and on the edge of the most ridiculous sense of excitement. But there Raffaele stood, sheathed in black jeans and a black shirt, tall, powerful and strong, and the very air in the cabin hummed with the vibrant energy that he radiated. He had been waiting for her to emerge.

'Don't keep me in suspense,' he told her.

Maya blinked in astonishment as she realised that he had somehow guessed exactly what she had been engaged in doing. 'How did you guess?'

'You stopped drinking wine two weeks ago. You've been feeling dizzy. You went to a lot of trouble to make elaborate excuses about why you wanted to visit a pharmacist yesterday. *And* I watch you like a hawk,' Raffaele countered with a wry smile. 'It's a *yes*, isn't it?'

'At least you didn't put a spy camera in the bathroom,' Maya breathed, her clear gaze pinned to his lean, darkly handsome face and the smile already pulling at the corners of his beautiful stubborn mouth. 'Yes, I'm pregnant…'

'I didn't expect it to happen so fast,' Raffaele confessed then, crossing the cabin in one long stride to reach for her, linking his arms loosely round her shoulders as he gazed down at her. 'How do you feel?'

'Excited, weird, pleased, all sorts of crazy things.'

'You're happy?'

'Yes. I love babies,' she admitted a little self-consciously.

'And why shouldn't you?' Raffaele replied lightly.

'How do you feel about this?' she pressed with intense curiosity.

'Delighted,' Raffaele said quietly. 'I wrongly assumed that this result would take a lot longer to achieve.'

And at least one of the happy bubbles inside Maya burst because 'achieve' wasn't the kind of word she wanted him to use. It wasn't an emotional word; it was a businesslike word that went best with other words like target and goal. It was a reminder that she wasn't in a typical marriage, a reminder that, indeed, her marriage as such was probably already winding to an end even as they spoke because that had been what they had agreed.

'And now you've got your freedom back just like you wanted,' Maya pointed out, because she could not resist the urge to speak out loud her greatest fear. She would get used to the idea that he was no longer a real part of her life, she told herself fiercely; she would forget that he had ever begun to mean something more to her.

Raffaele tensed, stunning dark golden eyes suddenly narrowing and veiling, curling black lashes concealing his expression. In silence, he nodded, a faint frown line etched between his ebony brows. 'It's a little soon to be thinking like that,' he murmured tautly. 'In fact, it's kind of insulting. I have more respect for you than you seem to think.'

But Maya wanted much more than respect, she thought painfully, hoping that what she felt for him wasn't really love but some lesser affliction like a teenager's overwhelming crush, which could often be short-lived. She could swiftly recover from a crush, after all. For the sake of her own peace of mind, she knew that she had to start moving on from their relationship as fast as she could.

CHAPTER SEVEN

BARELY FORTY-EIGHT HOURS later, Maya suffered a miscarriage.

The day before, Raffaele had insisted that she should see a Greek doctor to have the test result confirmed and have the usual health checks. Maya would've preferred to wait until they returned to London in a week's time but she had given way in the end because she wanted to follow all the rules. She had told the doctor about the incredible tiredness engulfing her and he had smiled and advised her that that was normal in early pregnancy.

That evening when they were sailing towards the island of Sicily, sheer exhaustion persuaded Maya into having an early night. Cramping pains in her abdomen wakened her after midnight and she sat up with a start, switching on the bedside light and pushing back the sheet to check that her misgivings were correct.

'What's wrong?' Raffaele demanded.

'I'm bleeding,' she whispered sickly. 'I'm having a miscarriage.'

In a matter of seconds, Raffaele leapt out of the bed and lifted the phone to wake his pilot and instruct him in urgent Italian. As if she were standing somewhere outside herself, Maya watched him as he pulled on jeans, reluctantly appreciating his extreme cool in a crisis and the way he took charge. 'There's no point in taking me to a hospital,' she told him ruefully. 'There's nothing they can do to stop what's happening at this stage of a pregnancy.'

'You *must* receive medical care,' Raffaele sliced in fiercely. 'And don't take that pessimistic attitude. It may be something else amiss, something that can be treated.'

He wouldn't let her go for a shower, wouldn't even let her stand up or walk. He bundled her up in a towel and a sheet and carried her up to the helipad where the helicopter was already powering up. Maya stopped arguing. She didn't need a doctor to tell her what had happened, and she knew how common early miscarriages were. Her baby, barely more than a tiny bunch of cells, was already gone. Rationally she knew that even then, but her brain was having a much harder time coming to terms with the knowledge.

The cramps became more severe during the flight and she struggled to hide the fact that she was in pain because there was nothing anyone on the flight could do about it.

Watching her, Raffaele felt sick and powerless, not sensations he was used to feeling. Her eyes were dark with strain in the white taut triangle of her face and her breathing was erratic, her hands clenching in on themselves. He knew she was in pain and he reached for her hand. 'Maya—?'

'I'm totally fine. Let's not fuss about this,' she told him briskly, snatching her fingers free of his and turning her head away, tears burning free of her lowered eyelids to trickle down her rigid face in silence.

Naturally, Raffaele didn't want her to lose the baby because that would mean starting all over again, she thought painfully. Just when he had been on the very brink of reclaiming his freedom, his neat little plan had fallen apart and they were being thrown right back to where they had begun. He couldn't possibly be feeling what *she* was feeling. The baby itself wasn't real to him the way it was to her. On *his* terms, their precious little baby had only been a means to an end, and she hated him for that, simply couldn't help hating him for it.

The helicopter ferried her to a private hospital in Sicily and she was whisked away from Raffaele. Once she had been examined and scanned, she was given pain relief and finally tucked into a bed in a quiet room where a doctor came to tell her what she already knew: her pregnancy was gone. She had thought she was prepared for that news, but it seemed that she was not and that somewhere deep down inside she had still cherished a dim and foolish little hope that her worst assumptions could yet be proved wrong. Only, unhappily for her, her pessimistic outlook had been correct.

And she felt gutted, absolutely gutted with hurt and disappointment. In the silence of the night, broken only by occasional quiet footsteps of the staff in the corridor beyond her room, she lay wondering if she had done anything that could have contributed to the miscarriage. Maybe she had eaten something she shouldn't have or caught an infection, maybe she shouldn't have had the occasional glass of wine after the wedding, maybe she had been too active scrambling over rocks and along goat paths in Raffaele's energetic wake while they were exploring, maybe her body just wasn't fit enough to host a healthy pregnancy. *Stop it, stop it*, her brain urged her as all the things she could have done wrong tumbled together in a crazed shout of self-condemnation inside her aching head.

It was so pointless to think that way because none of it could change anything: her baby was gone as though it had never been and that absolutely broke her heart. The tears she had struggled to hold back surged then in a blinding, stinging flood and she buried her convulsed face in a pillow to muffle her sobs.

'I'm so sorry...' Raffaele breathed stiltedly from the doorway because he knew how thrilled she had been about the baby.

In fact, he had been sincerely startled by her sheer enthusiasm at the idea of becoming a mother because the kind of women he usually mixed with invariably felt the need to deny the maternal urge as though it were a weakness or an unattractive trait likely to scare off eligible men. But not Maya, no, not Maya, who was who she was without fear or concern as to how she might appear to others and who wanted what she wanted without apology.

Tragically, he didn't know what to say to her and that felt like an enormous failing to him at that moment. He had spoken at length to the medical personnel, had heard every empty cliché that had ever been voiced on the topic of miscarriage and he didn't want to trot those same words out for Maya's benefit. *I'm sorry*, an expression of regret, seemed the only appropriate response.

In dismay at his appearance, Maya rolled over and sat up to focus on him through swollen eyes, angry resentment shooting through her in a heady rush of sudden energy. 'Of course, you're sorry…this development sets back your plans!'

'As of this moment I have no plans,' Raffaele intoned, moving forward, all lithe grace and self-containment. 'We need time to grieve.'

Maya looked at him and truly hated him. *Grieve? We?* She was an emotional wreck and he was calm and assured, which was only to be expected from a man who had no more feelings than a lump of concrete! As she tried to suppress the tumultuous surge of her resentment she studied him, her heart hammering somewhere in the region of her throat, it seemed, teaching her all over again, and when she least required the reminder, how weak she could be around him.

It was the middle of the night and, for once, Raffaele looked tired and under strain, the sculpted lines and angles of his lean dark features clenched taut and shadowing his dark deep-set eyes. But he also looked drop-dead gorgeous and vibrant as if no adversity could do him down for long. His bronzed skin still had the gleam of burnished gold like his eyes, his untidy blue-black hair remained glossy as silk, his arrogant head was high, the athletic flow of his lean, muscular body fluid. She wanted to reach out a hand to him and hold on tightly and she hated herself for that betrayal, for that need for comfort that made her so achingly vulnerable.

'This baby was never real to you the way it was to me!' she condemned bitterly instead. 'You didn't think of our baby as a little girl or a little boy, a child who would be a mix of us both, you only saw our baby as a device to be used to acquire a multimillion-pound company! You didn't see anything wrong with using your own flesh and blood that way! Even though you suffered because your parents broke up when you were a baby, it didn't bother you that you were cursing our child to grow up in a divided family as well!'

'You're right. I saw what I wanted and went for it. I've never had to think about moral boundaries or consequences such as this before and now that I have, I see that I went wrong. But I didn't realise that until I met you,' Raffaele bit out in a rasping undertone. 'Unhappily, I can't change anything I did now. It's too late.'

Maya wasn't even listening properly to him. 'Yes, too late,' she agreed sadly, lying back down and turning her face away. Aware of him hovering at the foot of the bed, she frowned. 'Go back to the yacht, Raffaele.'

'I'll get right on that,' Raffaele breathed through gritted teeth of restraint.

Was she kidding him? His wife suffered a miscarriage and she still expected him to just walk away? Getting it wrong wasn't an excuse to keep *on* getting it wrong. It meant he had to stop and think about what he was doing, but he didn't actually need to think about what to do next. Every fibre of his being told him that he needed to stay with his wife to support her after such a loss, even if she *didn't* want him with her.

It had been *his* loss too, he reflected, striding from the room and finding a corridor window that overlooked the car park to stare out. And he wasn't quite as callous as Maya appeared to believe because he too had been thinking about the child she carried as an individual. He had pictured a little boy with her fair hair and his eyes and then a little girl with his hair and her eyes, before accepting that genes weren't that easy to forecast and that their child might look more like one of their parents or not very like them at all. But the child would still have been *their* child, their flesh and blood. Not, however, a cross between a possession and a plaything, as his late mother had viewed him, not a sacrifice for financially foolish parents, as Maya had become. No, their child would have been safe from such unreasonable demands and expectations, their child would have been left free to become whoever and whatever he or she wanted within safe boundaries. Divided family or not, he would have made it work for their child, no matter what the cost.

But, regrettably, Maya was correct in that he had not started out thinking along balanced, reasonable lines that took a child's needs into consideration. He had simply seen an opportunity to expand his business empire and had leapt on that fresh challenge to alleviate his boredom. He hadn't cared about the position he was putting Maya in, nor had he thought in any depth about the child he was planning to bring into the world with her help. He had been selfish, callous, possibly even cruel, he conceded grimly, and he had few excuses to make for himself. He didn't need that technology company or Aldo's business holdings and properties because he was already richer than sin. He should have thought more than twice about dragging an innocent woman and a child into his bleak, self-indulgent existence.

All of a sudden he was no longer surprised that the situation he had created had blown up in his face. It was what he deserved, after all, for being irresponsible and lacking in compassion. But it wasn't what *Maya* deserved, he thought heavily, and Maya was devastated by the loss of their child. Maya had been ready to love that baby from the instant it was conceived. Her heart, unlike his own, was open and giving.

The dawn light was brightening the room when Maya wakened from her restless doze.

Almost immediately the events of the night flooded back to her and her eyes stung afresh, the heaviness in her heart weighing down on her again. A slight sound behind her made her flip over and stare in consternation at the sight of Raffaele slumped in a graceful sprawl of long limbs in the chair beside the bed. Unshaven with dark stubble framing his strong jaw line and accentuating his mobile mouth, he looked unnervingly familiar and precious to her. 'Why are you still here?' she exclaimed.

'Where else would I be?' he parried levelly. 'I'm part of this too. I couldn't leave you alone.'

'Even though I gave you permission to do exactly that?' Maya glanced away from him again, disturbed by how welcome she found his presence and the sense of security it gave her. The gut reactions Raffaele stirred were misleading and annoying. She always wanted to trust him even when she knew she shouldn't.

'You don't always know what's best for you,' Raffaele fielded.

'And you *do*?' An embarrassed flush lit her heart-shaped face as she heard the edge of scorn lacing her voice.

'I think we both know that if I had ever once considered what was *best* for you, I would never have met you in the first place and offered you the choice that I did,' Raffaele countered drily, sharply disconcerting her.

Maya stared at him in astonishment. Even if he had chosen not to approach her, her family's debts would still have been called in. Aldo would have seen to that. Her parents would have been made bankrupt and homeless and that was not a development she could have faced any more easily. Raffaele had given her a choice. It might not have been a choice she relished but at the time it *had* seemed the lesser of two evils.

'I suppose you never thought of something like this happening,' she muttered.

'No, I didn't,' he agreed quietly. 'It didn't occur to me that I was taking a gamble on real life and that that is likely to be messier and less predictable than a business transaction.'

'But then you're too accustomed to controlling developments and people and it's made you reckless,' Maya murmured, her heart jumping in her tight chest as he looked up at her through his lashes, his eyes a butterscotch gold that were like a shard of sunlight against his bronzed features.

'When it's a question of how I've treated you, reckless is an acceptable criticism,' Raffaele bit out grudgingly, his lean dark face stormy at having to make that concession. 'I didn't allow for the human factor.'

Involuntarily, Maya smiled. It was only a small smile, just a slight turning-up at the corners of her mouth. 'Who are you and what have you done with Raffaele Manzini?' she quipped.

Raffaele stared steadily back at her, his attention lingering on that unexpected hint of a smile, his golden eyes suddenly ablaze. With disconcerting suddenness, he vaulted upright. 'Would you like something to eat or drink?'

Heat had engulfed Maya, shocking her, her face burning up as she shook her head and reached for the glass of water beside the bed to raise it to her taut mouth, so unsettled was she by the effect he could have on her at the most inappropriate moments. 'I'm not hungry yet…probably all the medication. You should return to the yacht.'

'I'm booked into a hotel near here,' Raffaele slotted in. 'It's more convenient.'

'Go and get some sleep,' Maya urged.

Raffaele tensed. 'We haven't talked about what happened yet,' he breathed tautly.

Maya paled. 'I really don't want to talk about it. I just want to leave it behind,' she confided.

Raffaele frowned. 'I don't think it's that simple, *bellezza mia*.'

'It can be,' Maya muttered. 'Talking about stuff doesn't always make it better. I'd confide in Izzy but I can't, right now. She's pregnant. If I told her what had happened to me, it would make her sick with worry and it would spoil the pregnancy experience for her. It wouldn't be fair to do that to her.'

'Why do you always put everyone else's needs ahead of your own?' Raffaele demanded in honest bewilderment.

'I don't, not always. I wasn't kind to you last night,' she pointed out guiltily. 'I'm sorry that I lost my head like that.'

'I can take a lot of hard hits without buckling,' he asserted. 'Particularly when I deserve them.'

But Maya was already losing colour, lowering her head back to the pillow with a sinking sensation as she recalled the dark hollow look in his gaze hours earlier when she had accused him of not feeling anything over the loss of their child. That look had stabbed her to the heart. She had hurt him. She *knew* she had hurt him, and her distress was not an excuse. The problem with Raffaele was that he hid everything he felt and she had made assumptions and learnt her mistake the hard way after taking out her grief on him.

Raffaele left the hospital with the sense that once again he was doing the wrong thing because he didn't want to leave Maya alone, even if it was what she seemed to want. He had plans to make though, he reminded himself. Maya needed a distraction and, whether she appreciated it or not, the time and the space to recover from her loss.

Later that day, Maya wakened at lunchtime to a room filled with flowers and magazines and a selection of her own nightwear available. Although she had little appetite, she ate the light meal that arrived for her because she wanted to regain her energy. She went for a shower, dispensed with the hospital gown and doggedly fought the sense of emptiness tugging at her. The loss had happened, and she had to deal with it. Without her agreement, her bright future, shining with the promise of her first child, had reshaped itself. Breathing in deep, she walked back into her room and stiffened when she saw Raffaele poised there, momentarily dazzled by the lustrous energising power of him as he swung round to face her, stunning dark golden eyes gleaming in his lean, beautiful face.

'Did you manage to get much sleep?'

Raffaele shrugged. 'Enough. Sit down. We've got plans to make.'

'The doctor's already been here to see me. We can try again as soon as we like,' Maya declared stiltedly.

'That idea isn't even on the table right now,' Raffaele countered with a level of incredulity he didn't try to conceal.

Maya blinked rapidly, surprise and disappointment flooding her because there was nothing that she wanted more just then than the chance to conceive again. 'What is, then?'

'We're heading back to London so that you can see your family.'

'We can't do that. They don't know about us.'

Raffaele studied her intently. 'They do now. I phoned and *told* them. No, I didn't mention what's just happened because that's private and nobody else needs to know about it. But I did tell your parents that we're married, and they want to meet me.'

So taken aback was Maya that her soft full

mouth fell open. 'You told them?' she whispered in astonishment.

'We'll see your family and then we'll go up north to see my father and his,' Raffaele completed with satisfaction.

'You seem to have everything organised,' Maya remarked stiffly.

Raffaele lifted the folder he had set down on the table and tugged some sheets out of it to toss them on the bed. 'And now that I've given instructions for the house on Aoussa to be demolished, I could do with some ideas for the replacement dwelling. The architect wants some ideas from us concerning preferences.'

'*Demolished?* You've started that already?' Maya exclaimed, wide-eyed.

'I hate the house. You were right: it has to go.' Raffaele lifted and dropped a shoulder with graceful finality. 'But I could do with some ideas about what to build in its place.'

Maya nodded slowly. She never knew what he was likely to do or say next and it was, she was learning, part of what made him so uniquely fascinating. He didn't think or operate within conventional limits as she did. He made decisions at nuclear speed, followed stray impulses, did what *felt* right to him and stood by it even if, ultimately, it turned out to be a wrong move. She supposed marrying *her*, planning a child with *her*, fell into that latter category and now he was focusing his energies on other things.

But *not* on conceiving another child, she registered in confusion, wondering what that meant and wondering why on earth she should feel weirdly rejected. Was it because she had somehow become attached to him? It wasn't love. It couldn't be love—she wasn't fool enough to fall for a guy in a temporary marriage, particularly one who already had to be thinking of her as flawed and unfit for purpose because she had lost their precious baby within days of conception.

Her brain buzzed with conjecture. What was *his* ultimate plan? What was the bigger picture? To work out Raffaele's goal, she had to start thinking as *he* did. And he was clever and calculating and unscrupulous. All of a sudden he was taking her home for a visit, restoring her to her family. Was it a guilt thing? Was he trying to undo the damage he believed he had caused?

Hadn't he already pretty much admitted that he should never have offered her the chance to marry him in the first place? And never have acted on the plan for them to have a child together? Was it possible that Raffaele was already working towards putting her out of his life again and reclaiming his freedom? And why did that fill her with a sense of panic rather than relief?

a child too. But Was it possible that Raffaele was actually working myself… putting her
out of the picture and recriminating by line
…? And why did she think she would accept
of basic pattern their ends?

CHAPTER EIGHT

THREE LITTLE GIRLS engulfed Raffaele in a
wave of giggling, chattering excitement. An-
drea was five, Sophie was three and Emily
was an adorable toddler with a mop of black
curls. And every one of them reminded Maya
of their half-brother, Raffaele, and tugged
at her heart with a wounding sense of what
might have been because, with their dark co-
louring, they gave her a very good idea of
what Raffaele's own children might look like.
Clearly, the Manzini genes were strong, for
Raffaele bore a striking resemblance to his
father, Tommaso.

'The girls are always like a mob of little
thugs with Raffaele, all competing for his attention at once,' Claire, a brunette in her early
forties, groaned. 'Luckily, they calm down
after a while, particularly once the presents
are open. I've told him so often not to bring

them anything unless it's birthdays or Christmas, but he doesn't listen.'

Tommaso's wife and Raffaele's stepmother, Claire, was a social worker with warm eyes and an even warmer smile. The couple lived in a rambling old farmhouse outside Newcastle and it was very much a family home, from the children's pictures stuck to the fridge door to the clutter that lay around the kitchen. Boots lay in a heap by the back door while piles of kids' toys filled colourful baskets by the wall.

'He does tend to do his own thing,' Maya agreed, accepting the beaker of coffee her hostess passed to her. 'Thanks.'

'He's very generous. He tries to stick to the budget I gave him *most* of the time,' Claire conceded wryly. 'He's fantastic with kids too, much more relaxed with them than he is with adults.'

That was true. Maya had been downright startled watching Raffaele's easy interaction with his little half-sisters. He was very good with them and clearly a man who enjoyed the company of children.

The two women watched the two older girls learn to ride their new scooters in the custom-built playground at the back of the house. After throwing a tantrum because she had not got a scooter as well, Emily had gone down crossly for a nap, still attired in one of her new princess outfits from the wardrobe of dress-up garments she had received.

Raffaele had provided the playground for his half-siblings with all its safety features and the canopied roof that allowed for its use on wet days. Claire had been very frank on the topic of money with Maya, explaining that she and Tommaso only accepted gifts for their children and preferred to maintain their independence, rather than take advantage of Raffaele's wealth and generosity. Across the garden, Raffaele was standing talking to his father, a still-handsome man in his fifties. The two men had the same bone structure but Tommaso was smaller and slighter in build.

'You know, Tommaso was convinced that Raffaele would never marry,' Claire confided quietly.

'My family were equally surprised by our marriage. We were crazily impulsive.' Maya trotted out the same story she had told her own parents and, of course, her mother had thought it was madly romantic because a hasty supposedly love-at-first-sight match mirrored her own courtship history with Maya's father.

'It's amazingly positive to think that Raffaele can do *anything* crazy,' Claire remarked reflectively. 'I used to think that, for his age, he was always a bit too controlled, a bit too sensible and when it comes to women... *well...*' the brunette grimaced '...you're the very first he's brought to meet us and those I've seen him with in the media were pretty... er, trampy, for want of a better word.'

'I knew I should've worn a short skirt and a plunging neckline to fit the mould!' Maya teased with a chuckle, relaxing completely in the other woman's candid company. 'Raffaele likes those sorts of clothes on me, but I *don't*.'

At the sound of her laughter, Raffaele turned his head to look at Maya, noticing with satisfaction the healthy colour blooming in her cheeks and the smile curving her mouth. Maya had been as pale and silent as a wraith after she left the hospital but over the past few weeks she had gradually begun to return to normality. Restored to the company of her family during a lengthy stay in London, she had blossomed, vitality and humour returning to her clear green eyes. Only with him was she still reserved and withdrawn. He thought it was tragic that he had had to resort to using the company of others to draw her out and to make her relax again. But it wasn't surprising, he acknowledged grimly, not after what had happened between them.

For the first time ever, he was doing what he *had* to do even if it wasn't what he wanted to do. He *owed* Maya and he always paid his debts. Maya with her curtain of silky fair hair, long lissom legs and delicate curves, who made no effort whatsoever to be sexy but who could make him rock hard with one playful glance. He shut down hard on that very physical thought, reminding himself that all he could reasonably do was *attempt* to redress the damage he had done before letting her go again. But, regrettably for him, letting go of a woman he still craved didn't come naturally to him. The biter had been bitten, he acknowledged grimly. He was no martyr, no penitent, he wasn't essentially a *good* man, but he would force himself to go through the motions because that was what she deserved from him.

'No, a woman capable of telling Raffaele where to get off is unheard of and exactly what he needs,' Claire opined with a grin. 'From what I've heard, he runs rings round most women. They're too impressed by who he is while you seem to treat him as if he's normal.'

'Which he's not,' Maya conceded.

'And he never will be with that dreadful background of his and all that money,' Claire sighed. 'But he still needs someone to treat him as though he is.'

Only, not necessarily *me*, Maya reflected unhappily, already somewhat stressed by having recently heard her twin's frank opinion of her marriage. Since Maya had told her parents about her marriage, she had spoken to her twin on the phone and given her the same story.

Unhappily, she hadn't felt able to tell Izzy the whole truth either, not about the choice Raffaele had given her, not about their parents' debts being settled with their marriage and certainly not about the baby she had willingly conceived and then lost. Maya refused to burden her pregnant, newly married sister with the disturbing facts of her own situation, deeming it better to let Izzy believe that she had tumbled headlong in love with Raffaele while working for him and had rushed foolishly fast into marrying him.

Ultimately, Izzy had been most shaken by

Maya's news only after she had acquainted herself with the online gossip about Raffaele. Izzy had called Maya back purely to raise the topic of Raffaele's raunchy reputation as a womaniser and refer worriedly to the unlikelihood, in *her* apologetic opinion, of such a male choosing to stay faithful on a long-term basis. Her fear that Maya could not possibly hope to find lasting happiness with Raffaele had been unmistakable. Evidently Rafiq, Izzy's new husband and the father of her unborn twins, didn't have that kind of better-left-buried sexual past. Well, bully for him, Maya thought ruefully as she went pink with discomfiture.

Truth to tell, after all, Raffaele's amazing versatility between the sheets was more of a colourful memory for Maya than a current event. Raffaele hadn't shared a bed with Maya, never mind actually touched her in any intimate way, since she had lost their baby, and that distance he had forged between them hurt and made her feel more rejected than ever.

They were based in Raffaele's penthouse apartment in London where they were occupying separate bedrooms. That had been *his* choice. In spite of Maya's clumsy attempts at flirtatious encouragement, Raffaele had made no moves whatsoever. It was as though any sexual attraction she'd had had vanished after her stay in hospital. Evidently he wasn't planning or hoping to get her pregnant again and he wasn't interested enough in her to even approach her for sex. What did that tell her? Well, all it told Maya was that, in Raffaele's eyes, their marriage was already over. He had changed from a guy who couldn't get enough of her into a guy who didn't even seem to appreciate that she was still alive and kicking.

And what about what *she* wanted? Well, that was a ridiculously complicated question, Maya acknowledged ruefully. Every time she looked at Raffaele, she knew she wanted him, and being shot without warning from a passionate relationship into a platonic one was a shattering shock to the system. Naturally, she had told herself that she shouldn't still be attracted to him. Obviously, she had told herself that she should be relieved that he didn't expect to share a bed with her any more. But the logical approach hadn't helped because during the weeks of their marriage, all those sunny lazy days exploring the Mediterranean, she had grown deeply, *illogically* attached to Raffaele.

How had that happened and did it really matter that she didn't know *how*? The reality was that she had fallen in love with Raffaele. His dysfunctional childhood and his experiences since had made him cynical where she was naïve and too trusting; his droll take on his life, born out of those experiences, was nonetheless very entertaining and he often made her laugh. She had also learned that nobody could be kinder or more caring than he. But most of all, on the day he'd told her about his dogs being shot she had caught a glimpse of the broken-hearted, lonely, unloved boy inside him, of the terrible damage done to him and the lingering vulnerability that he worked so hard to hide from the world. And that had been that for Maya: her heart had opened up and taken him in and she knew she would fight like a lioness to protect him from hurt.

Yet *she* had hurt him at the hospital, reminding him of their unlovely beginnings and the child he had persuaded her to conceive to seal a business transaction. And she had seen him acknowledge the wrong that he had done, had witnessed the deeper understanding that he was developing and the care and support he was so determined to give her. She had grasped then that, in many ways,

Raffaele had been a case of arrested emotional development ever since his disturbing childhood experiences and now, finally, he was emerging from that shell to change and grow as a man. At the same time, though, she suspected that he was finding the emotions assailing him now almost as confusing and unsettling as she had once found his former emotional detachment.

It was mid-evening when they returned to the London penthouse. They had eaten on the flight back and Raffaele strode off to his room, leaving Maya marooned in the vast reception area with its sumptuous seating and fantastic view of the London skyline as night fell. She had never felt more alone in her life than she did at that moment, wondering why he was avoiding her, barely speaking, wondering why she didn't have the courage to reach out and demand answers from him. Because she was afraid, she accepted numbly, because she was afraid of hearing the truth that their marriage was over. And once Raffaele said those words, he would be free to leave and stay at one of the many, many properties he owned across the world instead. Once he was gone, he would be gone for ever and the very thought of that simply terrified her...

and yet, it shouldn't, it *shouldn't*. It would be a return to the life he had taken her from, and she couldn't face the emptiness of that again. She hadn't even known how empty her life was until he'd entered it.

'I'll see you…later,' Raffaele murmured from behind her. 'Probably tomorrow as I won't be back early.'

Maya unfroze with a jerk and glanced across the room at him, shot rudely from her reverie. He had changed into an exquisitely well-tailored suit, a dark claret-shaded shirt with an expensive sheen open at his bronzed throat. 'Where are you going?'

His sculpted mouth compressed. 'Out… I need to go out. I'm feeling…' he shifted a fluid brown hand in almost aggressive emphasis '…cooped up here.'

Already pale, Maya snatched in a deep quivering breath. 'Fancy some company?' she heard herself ask like an over-eager schoolgirl.

Stunning dark golden eyes rich as caramel, Raffaele tensed, his strong jaw clenching. 'Not tonight, I'm afraid,' he told her levelly. 'Tomorrow, we'll talk… OK?'

No, it wasn't OK. Maya didn't want him to go out, didn't trust him to go out in the parlous state of their already broken marriage. She didn't want to be around for the talk he had mentioned either. In fact, she wanted to run and keep on running from that possibility because, unhappy though she was with the current state of affairs, it was infinitely better than being deprived of him entirely. And not only did she not recognise herself in those cowardly reactions, she hated herself for that urge to shrink away and hide from a truth that would hurt.

As Raffaele disappeared into the lift, Maya lifted her phone and stabbed a single button. 'Sal?' she asked as the head of Raffaele's security team answered. 'I need to know where Raffaele is going tonight.'

Troubled silence fell on the line. 'Mrs Manzini...'

'*Please*... I don't want him to do something stupid!' Maya gasped.

And Raffaele was perfectly capable of doing something stupid to break himself out of the marriage he felt trapped in. It wasn't the confinement of the apartment that was making him feel cooped up; no, it was the constraint he had put himself under since she had left the hospital.

'I'll text,' Sal breathed curtly.

'I promise I won't tell him how I found out,' Maya murmured gratefully.

Within minutes the text came, naming a fashionable nightclub that Raffaele owned. And as Maya headed for her room, a voice was screaming in her head that she couldn't do this, couldn't run after him, couldn't force a showdown because that wasn't the dignified way to deal with a husband who didn't want to be a husband any more, who had probably never wanted to be a husband even at the start. But as stubborn, defiant and tough as Raffaele was, he was also still *her* husband.

Maya cursed as she rampaged through her elegant and restrained wardrobe because in the mood she was in, she didn't want elegant and restrained. She dug out the outfit Raffaele had bought for her that first day and wrinkled her nose at the leather and lace corset top and the tight skirt before throwing both items out onto the bed. If that was what he liked, that was what he was getting, she decided, pulling out sky-high heels and hold-up stockings before heading into the bathroom to do her face.

She needed to *do* something, not sit around wringing her hands being passive and letting Raffaele make all the major decisions. She was smart, she was strong and he did do crazy impulsive things, so she had to look out for him even if that meant sticking out a foot and tripping him up hard when he threatened to go in the wrong direction. He also needed to learn that she didn't play games, didn't close her eyes to avoid seeing what she didn't want to see and that she wouldn't dance around the truth when it came to laying down her boundaries.

When Raffaele saw Maya moving towards him in the club, his own security clearing a path through the crush for her benefit, he momentarily thought he was imagining her. How could Maya have found him? Why would she have followed him and why the heck would she be dressed in a way that was decidedly not her style? For some reason she was also sporting enough diamonds to sink a battleship. Maya, who was no fan of conspicuous consumption or showing off his wealth.

The short skirt put her outrageously long legs out on prominent display, legs that were incredibly shapely from slim knee to delicate ankle. Her round small breasts were swelling over the edge of the corset top in a most provocative show and Raffaele hated that he couldn't drag his eyes from her. With her hair draped like a sheet of pale satin down her slender back and framing her beautiful face, her green eyes were glittering as brightly as the diamonds in her ears and at her throat, her sultry peach-tinted lips slightly parted. And he knew right then, if he had ever had any doubt, why not a single woman who had approached him had contrived to awaken his interest. No man went happily from a woman who was a hundred out of ten in the desirability stakes and readily settled for less. In the seconds it took Maya to reach him, Raffaele's slumbering libido raced from zero to sixty, making his heart pound and his trousers tighten.

Rage shot through Maya the instant she saw Raffaele. He wasn't alone in his VIP velvet-upholstered booth, which was cordoned off from the rest of common humanity. Of course, he wasn't by himself, not a lone billionaire on the prowl for company. And when it came to company, Raffaele was surrounded by glamorous options. A half-naked redhead with all the chest development that Maya lacked was lounging up against the side of the booth trying to chat him up while stroking his arm, arching her spine back to ensure that her assets jiggled with her every excited breath.

An exotic brunette was coiled sinuously up with a giggling blonde on the seat beside him. Maya wasn't quite sure whether they were with Raffaele or with each other, but it didn't matter, he was still breaking rules.

As far as Maya was concerned, he wasn't allowed within twenty feet of a gaggle of sexy, beautiful women without her around or at the very least her permission. And no way was she giving him permission, not while they were married. The cordon was released to allow her free passage and Maya planted herself directly in front of Raffaele. 'Get rid of your friends,' she instructed quietly. 'Unless you want an audience to what I have to say.'

Spellbound by her belligerent attitude, Raffaele dealt her a slow, assessing smile and dismissed the company he had gathered. '*Madonna mia*... To what do I owe the honour, *bellezza mia*?'

'I wouldn't take that tone unless you want to be drenched by a drink,' Maya bent down to say.

Raffaele snaked out both arms and tumbled her bodily down on his lap. Maya fought that repositioning, which put her in a more submissive position, and wrenched herself over him instead, her tight skirt ripping at the split in the back as she knelt across him, green eyes angry and determined.

'What's the problem?' Raffaele asked, carefully smoothing down the torn skirt as best he could because he didn't want anyone else catching even a glimpse of her panties or her stocking tops.

Maya looked into gleaming golden eyes and spoke from the heart. 'We're married. You're exclusively mine and you're breaking the rules.'

'We don't have any rules now,' Raffaele argued tightly, struggling to suppress the bold arousal her behaviour had induced, wondering if there was a streak of crazy in his bloodline because he was finding her take-no-prisoners public confrontation the sexiest move ever. *You're exclusively mine.* Why did that outrageous statement turn him on even harder and faster? When had he ever wanted to belong to any woman?

'You only get your freedom back if I'm pregnant,' Maya reminded him. 'And I'm *not* pregnant!'

Sheer unvarnished shock reverberated through Raffaele's big powerful frame.

'And you're in default in this marriage contract too,' Maya added informatively. 'You're not even *trying* to get me pregnant.'

'In default? That's an…interesting take on the situation,' Raffaele conceded, seriously stunned by the dialogue. 'I wasn't aware that any further "trying" *could* still be on the agenda. In fact, for the first time ever with a woman, I was attempting to do the decent thing.'

'I don't *want* decent. I don't *want* apologies or pep talks or excuses from you. I want a baby,' Maya interposed bluntly. 'It's very simple.'

'Your grandfather can keep his technology company. I'm walking away from this unholy mess. I started it and I'm finishing it,' Raffaele stressed in a driven undertone.

'No, you're not. You don't get to make this decision for me. I still want a baby… *your* baby. Business doesn't come into this for me,' Maya protested. 'That company has nothing to do with this any more. Try to keep up, Raffaele…you're falling behind. If you try to walk away without fulfilling your obligations to me—'

'Obligations?' Raffaele growled.

Maya laced possessive fingers into his tousled black hair and ground down slowly onto his lap, discovering with secret satisfaction as she met the hard thrust of his arousal why he had been holding her off him. He wanted her, he was just fighting the urge and striving to hide his susceptibility from her.

He had married her, made her fall in love with him and given her a baby she had miscarried. Then in the aftermath, when she was at her most vulnerable, he had suddenly backed off, cruelly cutting the connection he had taught her to crave. Now all her hormones were in uproar and she wanted stuff she shouldn't want but couldn't help wanting. She loved him, she wanted him, oh, dear heaven, did she *want* him, and she also wanted another baby. Not as a replacement, because she would never forget the child she had lost, but she needed a child she could hold in her heart as part of them both after he had ended their marriage.

Big hands framed her hectically flushed face. 'That's *really* what you want most?'

Her eyes stung with tears, but she blinked them back fiercely, a feverish glitter in her green eyes. What she wanted most was his love but that wasn't a very likely development and she was willing to settle for the best she could get. Slowly she nodded in silent serious confirmation.

Raffaele crushed her soft mouth under his and kissed her breathless. And holy hell, he could kiss, she acknowledged.

Her heart was hammering so hard he could feel it against his chest. The hunger flooding him was overwhelming, almost unbearable in its intensity. This wasn't what he had signed up for but giving Maya what she wanted most was what he wanted to do. That felt right, all of a sudden continuing their marriage felt right instead of wrong to him and he consigned every other concern to hell. He had overthought stuff, reached the wrong conclusions, somehow forced her to come to him with a demand. But if it put Maya back in his bed, did she really think he had been likely to argue? And why, underneath the seething hunger he was experiencing, did he feel hollow, even disappointed, when he should be on a high?

CHAPTER NINE

'YOU DON'T NEED to carry me!' Maya scolded as Raffaele scooped her into his arms to carry her out of the limousine into the lift Sal already had waiting for them.

'Your skirt's ripped. I don't want you flashing those beautiful legs for anyone but me,' Raffaele whispered, his mouth close to her ear and lingering to tug at her soft ear lobe and then settle against the quivering pulse point on her neck that sent her temperature rocketing.

Maya had forgotten about that ripping sound she had heard. She was still in shock at the confrontation she had dared to stage and even deeper in shock at its unexpected success. Of course, Raffaele liked bold, he liked honest, he liked straightforward and that was what she had been, telling him what she wanted upfront, leaving no room for misunderstandings, keeping it simple. But there were still some questions to be asked, she reminded herself firmly.

He carried her into the master bedroom where he had left her sleeping alone since their return to London.

'Were you planning to sleep with another woman tonight?' Maya asked bluntly.

'No. I still feel way too married to consider any form of infidelity,' Raffaele admitted with convincing cool. 'I just couldn't face staying in tonight, so close to you and yet not being free to touch you. It plays on my nerves.'

'You're the one who settled himself into a separate bedroom!' Maya reminded him helplessly.

Raffaele settled her down on the bed. 'I thought I was being considerate. I thought the last thing you would want was me anywhere near you!'

'Why? It's not your fault I miscarried,' Maya countered gently. 'It happened and it hit both of us hard but I'm ready to try again... but you're not?'

'Once we were in the separate bedrooms it just seemed to make better sense to continue that way and let it all go,' Raffaele breathed in a raw undertone. 'I made a mistake forcing you into this marriage. I was trying to put it right as much as I could for your benefit.'

'I don't want better sense,' Maya whispered tremulously, welded to the scorching golden turbulence in his eyes and the amount of emotion he was struggling to contain, thinking yet again of how seriously she had underestimated him and his capacity for feeling and of how that could yet prove to be an insuperable barrier between them. Raffaele was feeling stuff again and he didn't like it: his frustration was palpable. There was no guarantee that once he came to terms with what he was feeling he would still even be attracted to her, was there?

'I don't want sense,' she said again. 'I just want you.'

But that definitely wasn't the truth, Raffaele thought grimly, gazing down into her anxious green eyes with a sharp inner pang: she didn't want him for his own sake. She wanted him to get her pregnant and ultimately, hopefully give her another baby. It wasn't that fine a distinction either, he reasoned, considering that any fertile man could have provided the same service. Even so, he would settle for it because he had never wanted any woman

the way he wanted Maya and living with her
without being intimate with her, he had decided, was an unbearable situation to be in
on a daily basis.

And if he had Maya back in his bed again,
life would feel *normal* instead of empty and
confusing again, wouldn't it? In reality he
suspected that it was that sense of normality, occupation and focus that he craved even
more than sex. And now he could stop agonising over such intangible responses because
they would soon die away again. Sex was
simply sex and Maya simply happened to be
the sexiest woman alive. Of course, it was
only sex with her that he was missing. Why
did he persist in seeing complexity where
there was none? She wanted a baby and, if
he was honest with himself, he did too now.
The child they had lost had marked him as
well, creating a space where once there hadn't
been a space in his world. There was nothing complicated about any of that, was there?
'You're exclusively mine,' she had said. That
was what had stirred up all the weird feelings infiltrating him. He didn't belong to her
and she didn't belong to him, regardless of
the rings they wore. But if another man so
much as looked at Maya, he would kill him.

That went without saying. That was normal, sexually possessive behaviour, he told himself calmly.

With a renewed sense of purpose, Raffaele gently turned Maya over and unzipped her skirt. 'I thought you didn't like this outfit.'

'I thought you did.'

'Oh, you put it on for me, did you?' Raffaele laughed softly as he unlaced the back of the leather top. 'Your seduction outfit? I like it even more. But to be brutally frank, anything you wear has the same effect on me. With you, I'm sort of basic in that field, *bellezza mia*.'

Maya tensed as he turned her back round to face him again. She gazed up at him, feeling that wild feverish flutter of excitement burning through her like a brand. 'Basic works for me.'

'It shouldn't. You deserve the flowers and the violins and the smooth stuff,' Raffaele told her earnestly. 'I wouldn't even know where to begin with all that.'

'You're doing just fine,' Maya breathed chokily.

'In the club,' Raffaele muttered raggedly, his nostrils flaring as he shaped his hands to the firm swell of her breasts, catching the straining peaks between his fingers, 'I just wanted to smash you up against the nearest wall and get inside you again. I was so turned on, I felt like an animal. That's what you *do* to me.'

A little quiver snaked through Maya as her nipples tightened and sent a darting arrow of heat down into her pelvis, making her shift, achingly conscious of the damp heat between her thighs. 'That's OK.'

'What would you know about it?' He wrenched off his shirt, angled up his lean hips to unzip his pants, vaulting off the bed to remove them. 'You've only had me...not the best introduction.'

'I like how you make me feel,' she told him confidently, determined not to hide from either him or herself when it came to that reality because he made her feel alive as nobody else ever had. It was as though she had gone through life sleeping until he came along, shattering her expectations but still somehow managing to steal her heart.

Raffaele closed his lips to a pouting pink nipple as he shimmied off her last garment, long fingers tracing the delicate folds between her thighs, and her head fell back and she gasped, hips rising in supplication, her whole body tingling with thrilling arousal. Slender fingers lacing into his black hair, she dragged him up to her and found his mouth again for herself, hungrily, urgently tasting him.

Arranging her beneath him, he drove into her hard and fast, stretching her with his length and girth. A rippling shockwave of delight convulsed her womb. It was electrifying, demanding, everything her desperate body craved. He delivered with every forceful thrust of his lean, powerful body until she was riding wave after wave of sensation. It was no gentle reintroduction to their intimacy; it was wild and elemental and incredibly exciting. He shot her to an explosive climax that sent pulsing paroxysms of pleasure rolling through her and she came back from that slowly with his name still on her parted lips.

Afterwards, Maya gazed up into his lean, breathtaking face, the line of faint colour accentuating his exotic high cheekbones, the stubble outlining his wide masculine mouth, and then she collided with his dark deep-set eyes, a scorching sunset gold with satisfaction and her every thought died away.

'I feel better,' Raffaele confided, smoothing her damp hair back from her brow and then momentarily lifting back from her to gather her tumbled hair off the pillow and push it out of her way so that she could cool down. A wolfish smile slashed his beautiful mouth as he held her possessively close. '*So much better, bellezza mia.* Maybe you'll let me take you to visit your sister now.'

Maya tensed with discomfiture because it was far from being the first time that he had mentioned that ambition. 'No, *when* I'm pregnant again, not before. I can't see Izzy and not tell her about the miscarriage, but I can't upset her with that when she's expecting herself. If I'm pregnant again, it'll be OK.'

Raffaele frowned. 'I can't believe you're being so stubborn about this. I know how close you are to your sister and it may take a long time for you to conceive again…we don't know.'

Maya shrugged. 'I know but I didn't think you knew.'

'I've been educating myself,' Raffaele admitted with a hint of amused one-upmanship.

Maya paled. 'Because you're hoping it doesn't take too long? Because you want your freedom back?' she exclaimed.

'No. I want a baby too and, I've got to tell

you, I intend to put my *all* into the enterprise,' Raffaele announced, sliding over her, strong and graceful and very sure of himself, shifting against her to acquaint her with his renewed arousal.

Maya laughed in relief, overjoyed that he had warmed to the idea of a child as well, knowing that that would be a powerful link even after they parted.

And if he had been fire and fury the first time round, he was a slow sensual burn the second time, letting the waves of pleasure ebb and then flow and wash over her until she was reaching for the stars again in an exquisite release.

'I've been thinking,' Raffaele mused as she lay in his arms afterwards, scarcely able to credit that they were sharing the same bed. 'We need a house here in the UK.'

'The last thing you need is another house,' Maya told him gently, thinking of the many properties he had inherited from his mother, few of which he used on any regular basis. 'You already have this place—'

'It's not child friendly though. We have to think of that. We'll need outside space for a child to roam. I'll get onto the agents and you can start viewing country properties within easy reach of London,' he completed, his decision evidently made.

'*Me?*' she exclaimed.

'You don't like it that much here, do you?'

'It's OK.' Maya cringed a little at making that understated description of her palatial opulent surroundings and wondered if just living with Raffaele had already made her insufferably spoiled. 'It's a bit bland but it's central and convenient for you when you have meetings.'

'I'm thinking of you and our child in the future. It makes sense to get the house organised now.'

And the penny of comprehension dropped with Maya then and she felt as winded as if she had been punched. Raffaele was already planning the separation to come, even though it could take months for her to conceive again. What else could he be doing? He saw a future in which they would occupy two separate households, one for him here in the penthouse and one for her and their child safely set at a distance from his. A country house, which naturally he wanted her to choose because he wasn't expecting to be sharing it with her. She breathed in deep and slow to calm herself.

This was what she had signed up for, she

reminded herself fiercely as her eyes stung furiously and she blinked rapidly and forced a stiff smile. She had signed up for a marriage, a child and a divorce and, ultimately, Raffaele would stick to the rules. He was comfortable with limits and rules, particularly where relationships were involved. It was typical of Raffaele that he was already working out in advance where to rehome her like a pet he had outgrown. Why on earth had she got the impression that anything between them had essentially changed?

But in the two weeks that followed, it struck her that the ambience between them *had* changed and not for the better. The sex was off-the-charts amazing, but Raffaele was more distant with her out of bed. He was working incredibly long hours and she would see him at breakfast and occasionally for dinner but not much else. He urged her to make a checklist of requirements before she viewed any properties and she spent hours studying houses online to fill her time, discovering that it was anything but easy to find one that ticked every box. And then the inevitable happened: she fell in love with a house.

'I don't understand why you want me to view this place with you,' Raffaele declared with an edge of impatience over breakfast. 'I don't care where I live as long as the usual facilities are available.'

'I would still value your opinion and, as the owners are abroad, you won't even have to make polite conversation with strangers,' Maya pointed out persuasively, wanting him to agree to spending some actual time with her that did not entail sex, wondering if that made her just a little desperate. He was following the rules of their strange marriage and she was trying to break the rules without him noticing.

With a groan, Raffaele agreed while reminding her once again not to organise any viewings for over the weekend.

'I haven't forgotten,' she told him a little tartly. 'You still haven't told me why—'

'It's a surprise. I'll tell you later,' Raffaele parried. 'After you've done a pregnancy test.'

Maya paled at the suggestion. 'It's too soon.'

'No, it's not and you're getting all stressed out over it, which isn't good,' Raffaele countered. 'We could be doing this for months, so let's not make a production out of a simple check. Months... *Madonna mia*...how will I stand all that sex?'

Maya went red as fire. 'Raffaele...'

Raffaele dealt her a wolfish grin. 'I can take everything you can throw at me,' he teased. 'Now give me the brochure for the house.'

Raffaele was picking holes in her choice even before they boarded the chopper that would ferry them to Grey Gables.

'It's at the very limit of a convenient distance from London,' he warned her.

'It's historic,' he pointed out. 'You said you wanted to avoid that because it's a protected building, which makes alterations difficult.

'It's also going to need more bathrooms and you said you didn't want anywhere requiring building work,' he reminded her annoyingly.

'It's got woods, acres and acres of woods,' he commented.

'Didn't you ever want to build a tree house when you were a kid?' she gibed in frustration.

'My play properties were built for me,' Raffaele admitted. 'And I would never have got to run free in the woods because Julieta would have deemed that, like a tree house, too dangerous. She had a whole list of pursuits which I wasn't allowed to follow and places I wasn't allowed to go…her control only loosened after I started boarding school.'

'Yes, but we're not going to be the same with our child,' Maya pointed out brightly, wishing she hadn't mentioned anything to do with his childhood with his troubled mother because that only roused unhappy memories.

Raffaele sent her a sardonic smile and handed the brochure back to her. 'And presumably, you're planning to give me triplets at the very least. Grey Gables has an awful lot of bedrooms.'

'But you'll need those rooms for extra bathrooms,' Maya tossed back, lifting her chin.

A couple of hours later, Raffaele watched as she toured the house while the agent waited outside to give them some privacy. Maya's hair was in a long golden braid, as rigidly contained as she was, slender shapely legs outlined in casual cropped jeans mounting the stairs. She was beautiful, so beautiful, her delicate profile absorbed, her soft mouth still unnaturally taut because he had dared to mention the pregnancy test they had agreed to do every month. Her entire focus was on conception, which was why he was praying that it simply happened, and quickly, to take that complication off the table. Once that was achieved, she would relax, open her eyes, maybe even see what else was on offer…

Raffaele studied the gracious landing, ancient polished boards creaking beneath his feet. Grey Gables was pretty much everything he had avoided throughout his life but that didn't mean that he couldn't see the appeal of the Georgian gem set within its own estate. It was, primarily, a *family* house with a warmth that even he could feel. The owners were downsizing, their children long since grown up, but happy snapshots of the life they had led at Grey Gables, fashionably presented in black and white, abounded. Maya, predictably, paused again and again to study the photos because that was what Maya wanted even if she didn't know it: she wanted a family life, a happy, perfect family life like the one she had grown up with. It galled him to acknowledge that truth but there it was. Maya's debt-ridden parents had still, against all the odds, contrived to raise happy kids.

'So, what's this surprise you won't tell me about?' Maya pressed as she stood at one of the windows in the master bedroom, which looked out across the front lawns.

The main bedroom was a beautiful room in a very elegant house with the delicate ceiling and wall mouldings and gracious marble fireplace still intact. She had already pictured the bedroom with that fire lit on a winter evening and she bit down hard on her lip when she registered that she was imagining Raffaele by her side. By the time winter came, she would very probably be pregnant, and he would be long gone, only reappearing after their child was born. Her heart clenched as if someone had squeezed it and she forced herself to focus on the view instead. Beyond the window, she could see long stretches of well-maintained lawn surrounded by towering graceful lime trees. Their weeping branches of bright green leaves almost touched the ground and beyond the formal gardens stretched a dense belt of natural woodland.

Raffaele strode across the room, opening doors, glancing in at a superb well-appointed bathroom and a pair of formally fitted-out dressing rooms, which she had already inspected. 'At least they didn't stint on the details,' he commented grudgingly.

Maya studied him. Even in faded designer jeans and a shirt, he still contrived to take her breath away at a glance. Nothing he wore said billionaire, aside of the slender gold watch on his wrist and possibly his handstitched shoes.

His whole attitude of masculine command and expectation, however, screamed his exclusive status for him. She had seen the female agent's fluttering, hair-tossing instant reaction as Raffaele had vaulted out of the chopper that had brought them to the estate and then paused to lift Maya out with the care he always utilised around her. The agent had had that glazed expression that women often wore in Raffaele's presence.

He was drop-dead gorgeous from his lean, powerfully built, hard body to his chiselled, breathtaking features. All that and money *too*, she had seen the woman thinking as she'd scanned him before staring at Maya as if trying to penetrate the mystery of how Maya had captured such a husband. No mystery, Maya had felt like saying, more of a trap sprung by Aldo, who had made both of them victims.

Raffaele could never just stand still in business. He had a great need to prove himself even if that meant competing against his own best performances year on year, and the prospect of anything new or challenging, like the current underperformance of her grandfather's technology company, had grabbed his interest and held him fast. Maya, in comparison, had become the victim of the belief that she could save her family without harming or changing herself. She thought it was fair to say that neither she nor Raffaele had appreciated quite what they were getting into when they had married. They had thought they could do it without pesky feelings and personalities getting involved and both of them had got it badly wrong.

'The surprise, Raffaele,' Maya prompted a second time, hitching a fair brow in emphasis.

Raffaele lounged back fluidly against the door frame and in that one sleek, graceful movement ensured that her fingers literally tingled with the desire to touch him. She wanted to trail her fingers through that tousled silky black hair, trace the sensual line of that full lower lip, smooth her hand down over his tightly muscled abdomen. 'We have guests coming this weekend.'

Maya struggled to drag her brain back out of the gutter, where his extraordinary physical pulling power had taken her. 'Guests?' she queried in surprise.

'We're holding a big family reunion,' Raffaele extended with a twist of his shapely mouth.

'You don't have family... I mean, apart from Aldo and your father, and London is too far for Aldo to travel,' Maya remarked, her smooth brow furrowing.

'*Your* family,' Raffaele corrected silkily. 'Your Parisi grandparents, your own parents and siblings. All of them are eager to have the chance to get to know each other.'

Maya blinked in bemused disbelief. 'And you just decided to go behind my back and arrange this reunion?' she exclaimed in disbelief. 'Without even discussing the idea with me first?'

'Your grandparents approached me. Someone had to step in and sort things out, although I can't take the kudos in this case. Rafiq, Izzy's husband, contacted me first.'

Maya froze in dismay at that admission. 'Why? Why would Rafiq contact you?'

Raffaele dealt her a pained look. 'Your twin's been worrying about why you haven't visited her or asked her to visit you. You've made a lot of ridiculous excuses and naturally she's worked out that you're avoiding her.'

'I haven't been avoiding her!' Maya raked back at him angrily, outraged that he had got himself involved in something that had nothing to do with him. 'My relationship with my sister is none of your business!'

'I'm not standing by while you endanger a

relationship that I know is very important to you, just as Rafiq wasn't prepared to stand by and ignore Izzy worrying that *she's* done something to upset you. I told him about the miscarriage.'

Maya stiffened, all the colour draining from her shocked face. 'You had no blasted right!'

'And he immediately understood why you'd been keeping your distance and why you didn't want to share that experience with Izzy right now. He won't reveal your secret. If it's any consolation, he believes you made the right choice even if I don't. Of course, he's looking at the situation from Izzy's point of view, but I'm looking at it from *yours*.'

'You don't know what you're talking about!' Maya slammed back at him tempestuously.

'I know you're still hurting and that your sister's support might have helped you to adjust. And don't tell me that I don't know what I'm talking about when I do,' Raffaele warned her grimly. 'But don't worry. Izzy hasn't been told and she won't be told unless you choose to tell her. Instead, I've taken the fall to explain your unavailability in recent months.'

'You've taken the fall?' Maya repeated blankly. 'What on earth are you saying?'

'That with Rafiq's agreement, he will inform Izzy that you've been avoiding her because our new marriage has been rocky and you didn't want her to see us together and notice anything wrong and start worrying about you,' he extended curtly. 'It's a good cover story and you can see her tomorrow evening.'

'Tomorrow?' Maya gasped in disbelief. 'Izzy's arriving *tomorrow*?'

Raffaele nodded confirmation. 'In advance of your grandparents. They're arriving the following day. And you can rubbish me in the husband stakes to your heart's content with Izzy. I'm not that sensitive,' he declared curtly.

'I'm not going to be rubbishing anyone!' Maya protested, moving restively off one foot onto another, shaken at the knowledge that she would be with her twin again after months of being deprived of her company. She was torn between joy at the prospect and rage with Raffaele for intruding. 'You shouldn't have interfered.'

'You were making a mistake and you didn't give me a choice.'

'I'm not *still* hurting!' Maya proclaimed

hoarsely, her green eyes flashing a defiant challenge.

'Yes, you are, *bellezza mia*, and so am I. That's completely normal,' Raffaele murmured sibilantly, curving an arm to her rigid spine and urging her out of the room.

Her clear eyes prickled. 'You—?'

'*Sì*. I may have got with the programme when it was a little too late but…' Raffaele shrugged a shoulder wordlessly. 'Let's walk through the grounds now.'

Consternation gripped Maya as it occurred to her that her refusal to talk about the miscarriage had also denied Raffaele any way of expressing his feelings, *his* grief. She had hugged her sadness to herself, excluding him, and that knowledge filled her with regret.

'I *can't* tell Izzy,' she whispered apologetically. 'She would be so hurt for me and I'm used to protecting her. I'm used to being the strong one.'

'It's your decision, but she's got Rafiq now and I have the feeling he would stand in the path of a tornado to protect her. You need your family, Maya. You'll need them in the future when we're no longer together,' he bit out in a harsh undertone.

And at those words, Maya broke out in a

cold sweat all over her body. She felt sick and dizzy and she pulled away from him to hurry into the cloakroom off the main hall before she disgraced herself. Her head was pounding fiercely, her stomach heaving but, luckily for her, she made it in time and for long moments afterwards, having bathed her clammy face and freshened up as best she could, she rested her brow against the cold tiled wall and breathed in slow and deep in an effort to calm herself down.

When we're no longer together.

He had said it, he had put it into words that could not be unsaid, words that cut through her like slashing knives. He had said out loud what she could not even bear to think about.

How very considerate of Raffaele to ensure that she had her family behind her for support when he walked away! She supposed that set-up would make his life easier, lightening up his conscience, if he would even have an attack of guilt at ditching her. And why would he? Why would he feel guilty when she had *asked* him for another baby? She had made that choice, that plea, that *demand*. Thinking about how she had approached him in the club that night, Maya shuddered with shame and comprehension. She had used sex to hold onto him, hadn't she?

Yes, Raffaele might have stated that he also wanted a child now more than he had at the outset of their marriage, but she had been the one to fling herself brazenly at him in public, spelling out that he could have anything he wanted if he would only stay with her long enough to grant her that one burning wish. The heat in her face climbed even higher as she looked back over the past weeks.

Sex was the lowest common denominator in a relationship, and she had certainly made use of it, she acknowledged in growing mortification. She had spent those weeks engaged in frantically, feverishly swarming over Raffaele every chance she got, like some sort of sex fiend on a roll. And Raffaele had liked that, had revelled in that, of course he had. But at the end of the day, it didn't make her one bit more special than any other casual lover he had taken to his bed. And he would have been downright shocked, she suspected, had he realised that she had *lied* when she'd approached him in that club.

She had said she wanted only a baby, but that was the biggest, most barefaced lie she had ever told. In truth, she wanted him because she loved him, and she wanted him *for ever*. So, she had only herself to blame for the consequences of her behaviour. Raffaele was already envisaging their separation, putting into place the supportive family framework he believed she needed for that future event, not seeming to realise that absolutely nobody in her family was likely to have the power to glue back together the pieces of her broken heart and fix her...

CHAPTER TEN

'CONGRATULATIONS,' THE URBANE private obstetrician told Raffaele and Maya the next morning, when the nurse reappeared with the result and a smile of confirmation.

Maya shivered, suddenly chilled, as Raffaele's hand on her shoulder urged her down into the seat awaiting her. As she had performed a test for herself before leaving the apartment, they had already known that she had conceived again. It had taken all of Raffaele's considerable argumentative skill to persuade her that she also needed to speak to a consultant to deal with the secret fears she had not shared with anyone. Only her fears were apparently not as secret as she had assumed when Raffaele was so readily aware of their existence. It was true, sadly, this time around she was not as innocent, and she couldn't feel joy as yet and couldn't luxuriate in the result as she had before because she was far too afraid that something might go wrong again.

Dr Carruthers spoke at length with ease, determined to allay her very real concerns. A very early miscarriage, such as she had experienced, was extremely common. Indeed, he told her, it often happened before women even realised that they had conceived, so any statistics he quoted her were almost certainly inaccurate. She had no grounds to suspect that there was anything else amiss with her and should approach this new pregnancy without undue concern or stress. At present, he saw no reason for her to take any additional precautions. He was very reassuring and Maya left his smart consulting rooms on Harley Street with a renewed sense of confidence.

'Are you planning to tell your twin?' Raffaele pressed.

'Yes. Not about before but about this, yes.' Maya's glorious smile lit her beautiful face to radiance. 'I can share this.'

Raffaele slotted her back into the limousine and, without even thinking about the intimacy of the gesture, she reached for his hand. 'We're pregnant!' she said foolishly and then flushed with embarrassment.

'Guess that means I'm unlikely to get lucky tonight,' Raffaele teased, dark golden eyes gleaming with amusement.

'Oh, don't you believe that you get off that easily.' Maya laughed. 'My hormones are going crazy right now!'

'I bet you anything that tonight you'll sit up gossiping with Izzy until the early hours of tomorrow morning and forget that I exist. You have so much to catch up on and once your parents and grandparents get together with you tomorrow, you won't have much privacy,' he pointed out.

And that was when she tugged her fingers hurriedly free of his. What on earth was she doing? Clinging to him? Behaving as though they were still a normal couple? Why was she behaving that way when the instant that pregnancy test had shown a positive result their marriage, as such, had become redundant? How had she managed to forget that reality even for a few minutes?

She scanned his teasing, charismatic smile. He was pleased, undeniably he was pleased that she was pregnant again. Naturally, he was because that put his freedom back within view again. Now he was more concerned with getting her settled into a house he had no intention of sharing with her and ensuring that she was once again fully integrated into her family circle. That was to be her solace for his absence, his departure from her life. All of a sudden, Maya felt hollow, the temporary lift of joy in being pregnant again draining away when she was forced to face the prospect of losing the man she loved.

Raffaele was buying Grey Gables for her and he had offered a premium if the owners were willing to vacate the premises quickly. Earlier she had been over the moon that he was as impressed as she was with the property, or, at least, sufficiently impressed to overlook the disadvantages he had outlined. She had nourished foolish dreams about them sharing the house as a new family, dreams utterly removed from reality for that had never been on the cards for them, had it been? And in truth, once Raffaele left the picture, she wasn't so sure that she wanted to move out of London and be at a less convenient distance from her family.

'Where are we going?' Maya asked as she realised the limo had pulled up on a busy street.

'I wanted to mark the occasion. I ordered it weeks ago,' Raffaele admitted confusingly.

'I want you to be wearing it when your sister arrives.'

Her brow furrowed as she glanced up at the logo of the world-famous jeweller's showroom before she was ushered inside, across a quiet shop floor into a private room where she sank down on a chair.

'The occasion,' she prompted, registering that he was giving her another surprise and reflecting on just how much Raffaele enjoyed surprising her, treating her, *spoiling* her with spontaneous unexpected presents. It occurred to her that she would soon be surprising him with the purchase she had already made on his behalf in honour of his twenty-ninth birthday in just over two weeks' time. A little chill tickled at her spine as she recalled the gift that had seemed like such an absolutely brilliant idea at the time she had come up with it, but now she found herself wondering if she had got it right for him or if, in fact, she had actually got it very, *very* wrong. Maybe her gift would be too personal and unwelcome? An unhappy reminder of an experience he preferred to forget? Or a new beginning? Well, there was no point agonising over her decision, she conceded ruefully, because she had already booked and paid for the two puppies, which were being kept until the big day.

The jeweller attending them with the utmost discretion produced an emerald ring for their perusal, waxing with enthusiasm about its perfection, its cut, the simple design of the platinum and diamond setting. It was a magnificent ring. She watched numbly while Raffaele threaded the jewel onto the same finger as her wedding band. 'What do you think?' he asked.

'It's breathtaking…' It was also utterly enormous and she listened intently while Raffaele told her how he had tracked down the stone in a private collection where it had resided for a couple of centuries and how, after persuading the collector to sell it, he had designed the setting. 'It matches your eyes.'

'If I truly had eyes that colour, they'd be in somebody's collection too,' she mumbled in a daze, flexing her finger under that new weight, wondering if she would ever, *ever* understand Raffaele Manzini because he gave her so many mixed messages.

A ring was such a particular gift, literally laden with meaning to most people, and she stared down at the ring, which he had been so careful to place next to her wedding band.

'It…it looks like an engagement ring,' she framed hoarsely when she could finally unglue her tongue from the roof of her mouth.

'It's pretty. It suits you,' Raffaele informed her almost brusquely. 'And since you went with the love-at-first-sight story when you told your sister about our marriage, it will be more normal for you to have a ring.'

'So, this is like a prop to make us look more like a convincing couple?' Maya questioned, her delight in her gorgeous ring ebbing a little.

Raffaele frowned. '*Madonna mia*…of course not. We're way beyond that stage now, aren't we?'

Were they? Here she was waiting to hear when he was planning to leave her now that she was pregnant again and he was busy buying her a truly spectacular ring and putting it on her engagement finger and telling her that it matched her eyes. Raffaele definitely moved to the beat of a different drummer and, while she loved that impulsive, unconventional ability he had to utterly confound and fascinate her, sometimes that exotic individuality was just a little exhausting and unnerving.

'Could we go and…er…look at baby stuff

now?' Maya asked in a discomfited, apologetic undertone only loud enough for him to hear as they returned to the car, her emerald ring glittering on her finger.

'*Baby* stuff?' Raffaele repeated in seeming consternation.

Maya cringed inwardly and outwardly and went pink. 'I just sort of…er…wanted to look—'

'Of course we can go and buy stuff if that's what you want,' Raffaele told her smoothly.

'No…no, we're not going to *buy* anything,' Maya contradicted with an edge of urgency. 'That would be unlucky. No, we're only going to window-shop.'

'I'm not much of a fan and don't have much practice of window-shopping,' Raffaele confided gently.

'Well, then, you can just drop me off to browse. That's all I want to do…it's my treat for me,' she admitted tautly.

'I wouldn't dream of allowing you to treat yourself alone, *bellezza mia*,' Raffaele retorted.

In an opulent department store, Maya almost touched an admiring finger to a tiny pair of cobweb-fine bootees and her eyes stung, excitement flaring through her.

'Come on…let's buy stuff,' Raffaele urged with enthusiasm even while he fully understood her reluctance.

Maya swallowed the thickness in her throat. 'No, not yet…we're just looking,' she repeated, examining a delicate lace shawl with brimming eyes of wonder.

'It's going to be OK this time,' Raffaele told her confidently.

'Why do you think that?' she whispered, closing a hand over his to pull him away from the display.

'Gut instinct and the reality that lightning rarely strikes twice in the same place,' he murmured bracingly, disturbed by the anxiety she couldn't hide. 'We're going to be parents.'

Ridiculously cheered by that confidence that came so naturally to him, Maya laced her fingers into his and they returned to the penthouse. Maya had a dozen things to do. Raffaele might have organised preparations for her family's arrival behind her back but there were all sorts of little touches she could add to make her relatives feel welcome, like Izzy's favourite magazines in the bedroom, flowers for her grandmother, who adored white roses, and tissues everywhere for her mother because Lucia would probably be crying a lot at being reunited with her parents. Although the two women and her grandfather had been talking on the phone in recent weeks, there had been a certain constraint and nothing could take the place of a face-to-face meeting and a frank conversation.

Raffaele strolled into the bedroom and watched Maya get dressed. She was no longer self-conscious around him, which he enjoyed. The vision of her willowy figure as she donned fine lingerie held him fast. She was still wearing the ring and he supposed that was something to be grateful for. He couldn't concentrate, he acknowledged. He had put everything into place just as they had planned, just as they had agreed, and yet nothing felt right. How could it when he was accustomed to having Maya in his life? Accustomed for the first time ever to sharing everything with another person? That was a huge change in outlook for him. Familiarity did not always breed contempt, as he had once thought it unerringly did with him and women. Disturbingly aware of the teeming turmoil he had been suppressing deep in his mind for weeks, Raffaele turned his brain to a more current topic.

'Has it occurred to you that Izzy's hus-

band could have settled your family's financial problems for you?'

Much struck by the concept, Maya rested
wide eyes on him. 'Seriously?'

'Oil-rich, future King of Zenara?' Raffaele
prompted gently. 'If you had turned to Izzy
for assistance you would never have met me
and never have married me.'

'But I didn't know about Rafiq then, who
he was, how rich he was or that they were
getting married,' Maya pointed out prosai-
cally, but she was involuntarily shocked at
the picture he had drawn. 'I had no idea that
she might ever be in a position to help. That
possibility never even crossed my mind.'

At the same time the very suggestion that
she might never have married Raffaele shook
her rigid. He had shaken up her and her life,
but she couldn't have unwished him, couldn't
bear the possibility that she might never
have known him. She tugged another pair
of cropped jeans from a drawer and teamed
them with a casual sleeveless top, sliding her
feet into comfortable mules.

Before Izzy arrived, Maya questioned
whether she should admit to being pregnant,
lest something go wrong again. And then she
scolded herself for that pessimistic thought

and reminded herself that she could not live her life that way, always expecting the very worst things to happen to her. After all, Raffaele had happened and, while losing him would be bad, she could not regret learning to love him, could not regret anything they had shared and, least of all, the child they had conceived.

Izzy arrived in a welter of buzzing chatter. Maya barely got time to meet her brother-in-law, Rafiq, before Raffaele bore him off into his home office to give Maya and her twin some privacy. Izzy hugged her and bounced around the room, full of energy, the proud curve of her pregnant stomach already obvious.

'Twins,' Maya remarked in awe.

'I know. I still can't believe it!' Izzy exclaimed with a grin. 'Rafiq thinks I'm a living miracle, which is rather nice.'

'I'm pregnant too,' Maya whispered before she could lose her nerve again.

Izzy's eyes rounded in surprise and delight and then she closed her arms around her taller sibling with unashamed affection. 'Wow…that's clever timing. I wasn't expecting *that* news! My goodness, now we'll be able to share stories every step of the way.'

'I'm only just pregnant,' Maya confided.

'Rafiq told me that you and Raffaele had been having problems,' Izzy murmured very quietly, her gaze troubled.

'Oh, that's in the past. Teething troubles,' Maya hastened to assure her twin. 'We probably rushed into getting married too quickly.'

'It was very sudden but, let's face it, when the connection is special, you *know* pretty soon,' Izzy burbled, her obvious anxiety ebbing at Maya's light tone and smile. 'I thought something was wrong and I was losing you.'

'You're never going to lose me,' Maya assured her fondly. 'I was thoughtless, trying to put up a front, that's all.'

And the evening ebbed away, almost without Maya noticing as she and her sister caught up on all the news. Rafiq and Raffaele joined them for dinner but had to make their own conversation. It was indeed the early hours before Maya finally crept into bed, sliding in beside Raffaele and hooking an arm round him, although there was really no need for her to move that close in the huge bed.

'Feeling happier?' Raffaele asked, startling her because she had assumed he was already asleep and wouldn't have slung that statement possessive arm round him had she known he was still awake.

'Yes,' Maya admitted freely. 'Much happier.'

Her parents arrived early. Her mother, Lucia, was very nervous, and Maya tried to calm the older woman down about her approaching reunion with her once-disapproving parents. Her grandparents arrived an hour later and the surprise they brought with them was her grandfather's niece, Aurora, a stunning blonde model, who had hitched a ride in their private jet because she had an assignment later that day in London.

'I'm so sorry for intruding but I'll only be staying for an hour or so. I did so want to take the opportunity to get to know your side of the family,' Aurora told Maya, easing past her rather as if she weren't there to concentrate her full attention on Raffaele. 'Hi… I'm the marriageable Parisi female possibility whom, sadly, you never even got the chance to meet.'

Stunned to overhear that low-voiced, teasing self-introduction, Maya turned her head to catch Raffaele's flashing smile of amusement. He liked bold, he liked brazen, he liked confident. A shaft of fierce jealousy pierced Maya and it was an effort to concentrate on her grandmother's sobbing reconciliation with her daughter and step in with the occasional soothing sentence and reassuring hugs.

While that was taking place, Raffaele stood across the room chatting to Aurora, a tall, leggy figure clad in a white dress that was the perfect frame for her even more perfect figure.

'She's flirting with him,' Izzy remarked in disbelief. 'What's she even doing here?'

'Apparently she's here to get to know *us*,' Maya said drily, relieved that her sibling hadn't overheard Aurora's opening sally to Raffaele because Izzy would've sought an explanation and the carefully drawn story of Maya's marriage would have fallen apart.

'Not making much effort, then, is she?' Izzy commented. 'Go over there and act like a wife. Warn her off.'

'I trust Raffaele,' Maya fielded stiffly.

But she didn't and the polite lie roused colour in her cheeks. How could she trust a man who wasn't in love with her? How could she trust a man whose right to freedom after she became pregnant had been written into their pre-nup? And there Aurora was, exactly the kind of glossy, self-assured woman whom Raffaele had specialised in before he married

Maya. Maya watched Aurora toss her long, unnaturally pale blonde hair while treating Raffaele to flirtatious, covetous looks from her sultry brown eyes and she wanted to slap her and lock Raffaele in a cupboard where no other woman could get near him. Her mood swan-dived while her temper bubbled.

Maya's parents and grandparents decided to move their reconciliation to the Campbells' house. Lucia and Rory had to be home in time for Matt returning from school and the older couple were eager to meet their youngest grandchild. Izzy and Rafiq accompanied them and then planned to return to the hotel they had organised, Izzy explaining apologetically that she wanted to lie down and nap for a while. After a great deal more hair-tossing and giggling, Aurora departed as well, still as much a stranger to Maya and her immediate family as she had been on her arrival.

'It went well,' Raffaele remarked with satisfaction when their last visitor had departed. 'Fences all mended…and you and Izzy enjoyed yourself.'

'We did.' The silence smouldered. 'Would you have preferred to have married someone like Aurora?' That question just bounced off

Maya's tongue before she even knew it was there.

Raffaele dealt her a surprised appraisal and strolled back into the lounge. 'Why are you asking me that?'

Maya compressed her lips and gave a jerky shrug. 'She's definitely more your style than I ever was.'

'Realistically, I don't think it could ever have been a legal option because a niece isn't as close a relative as a granddaughter,' Raffaele fielded. 'When she made that remark, she was only trying to get a rise out of you. I think she's jealous that she missed out on what she would have seen as an opportunity to enrich herself.'

'No, she was jealous because I'm with you.'

'Then, she doesn't know what I put you through,' Raffaele parried. 'Your twin was watching me like a hawk while I was with Aurora. It's pretty obvious that she thinks I'm not to be trusted around other women. I hope that doesn't last.'

'It won't matter if it does, will it?' Maya cut in curtly. 'We'll be separated and you won't be my business any more and I doubt if there'll be any reason for you to meet my sister again.'

Frowning, Raffaele studied her. 'What are you talking about?'

'I get pregnant and then we split up,' Maya reminded him doggedly, choosing to voice her biggest, deepest fear as if throwing it into the open would magically dispel it. She shifted restively as her phone vibrated in her pocket. 'We agreed.'

Raffaele breathed in deep and slow, dark eyes flaring like fireworks. 'I'm not ready to let you go.'

'I thought you played by the rules. That was our business deal.'

'That deal ended in Sicily and we renegotiated,' Raffaele informed her.

'I don't remember renegotiating anything!' Maya slung back at him tartly.

'You came to my club and told me that I was *yours*,' he reminded her.

Maya coloured hotly at having that reminder tossed at her. Her phone vibrated afresh against her hip and with a muttered apology she dug it out and listened to the voicemail, waving her hand at him in a frustrated silencing motion as she tried to listen to the lengthy harassed message left for her. The breeder who had sold her the puppies had been taken into hospital for emergency surgery. The caller was the breeder's daughter and she was ringing to tell Maya that she would be dropping off the pups early because she was unable to look after them while her mother was in hospital. Dismay and disappointment filled Maya and she wondered how much earlier the puppies would arrive because she really had wanted them kept until the day of Raffaele's birthday.

'Why did you tell me that I was yours?' Raffaele asked with icy precision.

'I should think that would be obvious to a man of your intelligence.'

'Oddly enough, it's not,' Raffaele contradicted.

In a storm of turbulent emotions and growing mortification, Maya turned back to him. 'I'm not having this conversation with you right now... I can't think straight!'

As she stalked off towards the bedroom, Raffaele followed her. 'We're having this conversation now.'

'This is not the right moment to be dominant,' Maya told him shakily.

'I need an honest answer.'

'All right, I would have told you *any-thing* that night to keep you away from other women and get you home,' she admitted between clenched teeth. 'Happy now?'

'You mean…you were *lying* when you said that *all* you wanted from me was another baby?' Raffaele pressed hoarsely.

'Yes, I was lying. I was desperate. I was jealous and scared that you were going to go off and do something really stupid that there would be no coming back from,' she muttered in a bitter surge.

'If the "doing something really stupid" involves me going off with other women, that was never a risk. I don't cheat and I haven't wanted anyone but you since I first laid eyes on you at that hen party and you pretty much told me to go to hell,' Raffaele advanced rawly. 'I'm disappointed that you felt the need to lie to me about anything though. But why were you feeling *desperate* that night?'

The bell buzzed and she heard Sal's voice mingling with their housekeeper's, a strange low whining sound, the noise of something heavy being shifted over the tiled floor and a lot of exclamation from at least two male voices. And then the animal whines penetrated and she realised that the puppies must have been delivered and she shut her eyes tight, wondering what else could possibly go wrong in the space of one short day.

'I was desperate because I love you,' she told Raffaele flatly, assuming that that would end the humiliating dialogue. 'Having another baby was only an excuse to hang onto you. It was the only excuse I could come up with in the time I had. And you *went* for it. You went for the sex, which is OK…you *are* a man and you do like things simple. Excuse me…could you stay in here for a while? I have something to sort out.'

What on earth was she going to do with the puppies? This, the very day their marriage disintegrated, was *not* the moment to gift Raffaele a pair of dogs. But she couldn't ask the breeder's daughter or whoever was delivering them to take them away again because they were now Maya's responsibility.

She loved him.

She had lied to him only because she *loved* him, Raffaele reflected, thunderstruck by that admission. Even after all he had done, she had somehow contrived to fall in love with him? Rafiq had compared the conception of Izzy's twins to the eighth wonder of the world but Maya had pulled off an even bigger wonder in Raffaele's opinion. She loved him. He couldn't believe it, he just couldn't believe it and, intent on seeking further explanation, he followed her back out of the bedroom and down the corridor to where Sal and two of his security team were standing over a giant pet carrier, Sal's face pale and rigid.

'What's going on?' Raffaele prompted.

The strange woman beside the carrier broke into a flood of explanation that ranged from her mother's broken hip to her mother's current incarceration in hospital. 'I couldn't possibly keep them for you the way my mother promised,' she said apologetically to Maya. 'There's no room in my home for two lively puppies.'

'I understand. It's fine, thank you for bringing them,' Maya broke in gently.

'I'm afraid I'll have to take the carrier with me but I've brought a bag of immediate supplies, their vaccination records and current feeding schedule and their other documentation,' the woman told Maya, indicating the large sack one of the men carried as she bent down to release the catch on the carrier. 'Any problems you have, my phone number is in the bag.'

Maya caught a glimpse of Sal's anxious

face as she bent down and guessed instantly that he knew the same tragic tale of Raffaele's brief pet ownership as she did and was concerned about Raffaele's possible reaction to the animals. A little black nose poked curiously out of the carrier, swiftly followed by a little squirming golden puppy body, and then a second explorer appeared.

'They were a gift for your birthday,' Maya whispered weakly to Raffaele as the carrier was withdrawn. Somehow, she got through the departure of the breeder's daughter and said all that was polite before she even dared to glance in Raffaele's direction again.

Raffaele was down on the floor engulfed in puppies. At least he wasn't backing away or fighting them off, she told herself in consolation. He lifted glinting dark golden eyes to hers and smiled. 'Thank you,' he said in a husky undertone.

Maya recognised the tears in his eyes, and she was stunned. Grinning, Sal was already hustling the rest of his team out of the penthouse and their housekeeper was lifting the sack of supplies.

'Puppies,' she said in barely hidden consternation. 'Here.'

'But not for long, Mrs Abram. We're moving out to the country as soon as possible,' Raffaele informed her, a puppy gathered under each arm as he walked back to their bedroom, clumsily hit the button that opened the patio doors onto the balcony and set both little animals down outside. Puddles quickly appeared and he laughed. 'Yes, these two are going to keep us busy.'

'You're not upset?' Maya whispered worriedly. 'It seemed such a great idea but after I thought about what I had done, I started getting second thoughts, but it was too late because I'd already booked and picked and paid for them.'

'It *was* a great idea…and now I believe that you love me,' Raffaele admitted almost buoyantly. 'Because you understand me too. You knew I was afraid to love anything or anyone again.'

'Yes,' she muttered limply. 'You don't mind me loving you?'

'Why would I mind such an honour?' Raffaele demanded. 'If it means you'll consider staying with me for ever? I presume it *does* mean that? I've got you for good?'

Her smooth brow furrowed because she was confused by his attitude. 'For good?'

'We're not a business deal any longer, we're

a couple in a normal marriage. That's *all* I want and I can promise you now that I will not do anything to make you regret staying with me,' Raffaele swore feverishly. 'I'll probably annoy you and frustrate you at times, but I will never deliberately hurt you.'

Maya nodded slowly as if she was afraid to break the spell. 'For good,' she agreed. 'But what's changed?'

'I had the stupid idea that all you did want from me was a baby, that you didn't actually want me for me...which was perfectly understandable after the way I'd behaved. But it wasn't something I felt that I could live with long-term,' he explained ruefully. 'You could have had a baby with any man, even had a baby without a man and gone for artificial insemination, so you wanting a baby fathered by me didn't really mean much, just that you knew it was achievable with me because you already knew that I was fertile.'

Maya had paled. 'I never thought of it from that angle.'

'Nobody has ever wanted me for me but you,' Raffaele breathed grimly. 'I've been wanted a hundred times over for my wealth, my looks, my body, for the publicity I attract. I've never been wanted just for me.'

'Oh, I'm sure you have, you probably didn't notice,' Maya opined, dismayed to register once again that she had wounded him by telling him that she only wanted him because he could give her another baby. 'And maybe you haven't always been the most lovable person around other women, but you've been honest and wonderful with me since quite early on, always surprising me with how kind and thoughtful you could be, and tender.'

Raffaele winced. 'I'm really not the tender type.'

She wanted to tell him how amazingly affectionate and demonstrative he could be, but thought that possibly it was wiser for him to slowly recognise that about himself. He needed to accept that his ready affection did not in any way detract from his masculinity, that indeed it only enhanced it.

He had picked her a dream of a wedding gown, had guided her around Egyptian antiquities purely to surprise and please her, had in every way pandered unerringly to her likes and dislikes rather than his own. He had reunited her family, had introduced her to her long-lost grandparents and had searched out and designed a beautiful ring for her pleasure. He had even lied and declared that their marriage was rocky to his brother-in-law to cover up any damage she might have inflicted by avoiding her sister for so long.

And after they had been engulfed by their first crisis when she suffered a miscarriage, he had ignored her attempts to push him away even though that would have offered him an easier path. He had not been detached and even when she had lashed out at him, he had stayed supportive and caring. The more she thought about everything Raffaele had done for her since their first intimidating meeting, the less she marvelled at the love she had for him because he had changed just as much as she had changed and within that change they had grown very close.

'In fact… I may not be tender or sensitive or any of that stuff that's important to women,' Raffaele admitted gruffly, 'but I do really love you. I couldn't face the idea of life without you. When we viewed Grey Gables, I said, "when we're no longer together" to try and get a reaction out of you…something, *anything* that would give me hope, but instead you succumbed to the pregnancy sickness and afterwards, well, you were a bit quiet but you certainly didn't seem upset to me.'

'You said *that* deliberately?' Maya gasped.

'I was upset and hiding it. Where were your eyes?'

'Well, you're pretty good at hiding being upset. You burbled about the house all the way back here.'

Belatedly she blinked. 'You said that you loved me?'

'You're the only person I've ever loved. I like my father, my little sisters, but I don't think I love them. I don't think I've let myself love them, but I didn't get a choice with you. From the start I was flooded by these feelings about you and I was always burying them and then we lost our baby and...' Raffaele turned in an almost clumsy half-circle. 'Suddenly it was all there in front of me, how much I cared about you, how much it hurt to see you hurting and not be able to fix it for you. I felt helpless. I hated it at first. I was flailing around trying to work out what would be best for you, what would make you happy even if it made me unhappy and that's why I took you to see your family.'

'And that's why you stayed out of bed with me too,' Maya guessed. 'Because you thought letting me go was the kindest thing you could do for me...you idiot!'

'So, you stormed into the club that night and that was so incredibly sexy, such a turn-on.'

'You're easily impressed, Mr Manzini,' Maya teased, looking up at him with her heart in her eyes. 'And such a sweetie behind the nasty front. What did you really think of cousin Aurora?'

'Pushy, fake, not my type but she made you jealous and I liked that, which is why I stayed talking to her. I could see your annoyance,' Raffaele confessed ruefully.

'You can be *so* sneaky sometimes,' Maya sighed, wrapping both arms round him and resting her cheek against his shirtfront, loving the familiar warmth and scent of him.

He tilted back her head and kissed her passionately. 'I want you so much at this moment.'

'You can't have me. We have puppies to take care of,' Maya reminded him ruefully, watching the puppies gambol about the floor.

'All right, we feed them, we play with them, we come up with some names for them and then, we go to bed and they get an early night as well,' Raffaele proposed.

'We'll see. You're happy with them? They weren't a stupid gift?' she checked.

'This is my fresh start in life alongside you.

There's nothing stupid about that,' Raffaele assured her fondly, running a fingertip along her cheekbone and leaning down to claim another, longer kiss. 'I love you, I'll love our child and I'll love our dogs.'

It was late when the puppies got fed and several shoes got chewed up in the intervening time, but Raffaele and Maya got to make love and celebrate their newfound happiness and both pets and owners remained delighted with each other.

EPILOGUE

FIVE YEARS LATER, Maya lay back on her sun lounger in the shade with Izzy beside her.

It was gloriously peaceful on the little island of Aoussa. The children and the dogs were down on the beach with their nannies. Izzy was a queen but she didn't act like one in private because Maya was always teasing her about the fact.

Maya had given birth to a little girl called Greta, and she was blonde and dark-eyed and crazy about mechanical things. Maya had had an easy pregnancy and a straightforward delivery but she had been well into the second trimester before she'd stopped fretting about something going wrong again. A year later she had conceived twins and, like her sister, had given birth a few weeks early. She had had two little boys, Pietro and Daniele. Black-haired and green-eyed and identical, they were noisy little boys full of endless energy, she thought with a rueful smile, but wonderfully affectionate and loving. Izzy's family was complete with her two girls, Lucia and Leila, and her son, Nazir, and Maya rather thought her family was complete as well unless Raffaele took another notion and persuaded her otherwise.

Raffaele adored children, his own children in particular. He got out of bed at night when they were babies and got under the feet of their nanny. He changed nappies, built brightly coloured plastic towers of bricks and dressed dolls and combed their hair. He showed their children all the love he himself had lacked but he didn't over-indulge them.

The new house on Aoussa was a rambling ultra-modern property, perfectly suited to family occasions, which was fortunate when pretty much their whole lives revolved around family connections. The sisters got together as often as possible. Maya and Raffaele would fly to Zenara and stay at the palace in the desert with Rafiq and Izzy and their children would race around together kicking up a storm. As couples they got on very well. Maya had long since confided in Izzy about the loss of her very first pregnancy, but she hadn't yet told her twin the truth of why she had married Raffaele. She didn't think that would be fair to him when he had changed so much since then and she didn't want her sister to think less of him. She was as protective of Raffaele as she had ever been.

She saw a great deal of her parents and her grandparents because when she visited Izzy and vice versa, their older relatives were often included in the invitation. Her little brother, Matt, had benefitted hugely from the stem cell treatment and was no longer in a wheelchair but could now get around on crutches. His condition was still improving as he was still undergoing treatment. Raffaele's great-grandfather, Aldo, had died two years earlier and Raffaele regretted never having had the chance to get to know the old man better before his dementia set in. They saw Tommaso, Claire and Raffaele's half-sisters regularly as well.

Raffaele's giant business holdings had begun to take up too much of his time and when Maya complained about the long hours he was working, Raffaele sold off some of his empire, choosing to invest instead. Maya wrote a mathematics textbook, which only sold to very clever people but that didn't bother her. She had Raffaele, her children, the dogs, a large and demanding extended family and entertainment to organise, and in reality she didn't have time for much else.

Now, when she watched Raffaele striding up from the beach, the dogs, Luna and Primo, at his heels, Pietro plodding after his father with his thumb stuck in his mouth, Daniele lazily dribbling a football and Greta dragging her basket of toy cars and diggers behind her, she got to her feet. Behind the group, Rafiq was urging his children towards the house with the nannies in attendance.

There Raffaele was, vital and golden in swim shorts and nothing else, and her heart hammered like crazy inside her chest.

'The nannies are about to feed the tribe and we're…we're taking a nap,' Raffaele announced with a wicked gleam in his dark golden gaze.

Maya turned as red as fire.

'I thought only children need a nap in the middle of the day,' Izzy remarked pointedly.

'The heat drains Maya,' Raffaele countered cheerfully. 'If she doesn't get a nap now, she'll be asleep before we get the BBQ lit.'

Izzy rolled her eyes with amusement and said nothing more.

'Do you have to be so obvious?' Maya hissed as Raffaele urged her upstairs to their secluded bedroom suite, which rejoiced in a spectacular view of the sea and *Manzini One* moored out in the bay.

'You know you wouldn't have me any other way.' Raffaele laughed. 'I don't want to turn into a boring lover who waits for bedtime when you're most tired. No, I'd much rather have you sun-warmed and sexy and sandy, even if you're embarrassed by something as entirely natural as your husband lusting after you.'

'You're never going to be boring in bed or out of it,' she promised him lovingly.

'But that's because I've got you to keep me on my toes and fully diverted.' Raffaele watched her strip off her wrap and bikini and fold sinuously down on the bed, stunning dark golden eyes absorbing her every move. 'You're so beautiful. I don't want to be shallow, but that *is* the very first thing I noticed about you.'

'You're forgiven. It's the very first thing I noticed about you as well,' Maya confided as he sprang up on the bed beside her.

'You blew me off!' Raffaele reminded her

accusingly as if that memory still rankled. 'You walked away from me!'

'I don't think you'd have wanted me half as badly if I hadn't done that,' Maya murmured.

Raffaele strung a line of kisses across her collarbone and butterflies danced in her tummy, heat stirring lower down. 'You're probably right, but then I'm convinced that you were made for me, put on this earth just for me to love. Women don't come any more perfect than you.'

'I'm not perfect.'

'You're perfect for me,' he contradicted. 'That's why I love you...we fit.'

Maya trailed her fingers through his tousled wind-blown black hair, her gaze captured by his. 'Yes, we do,' she agreed softly. 'We fit amazingly well, don't we?'

'And I love you more every day, particularly when you agree with me,' Raffaele said with a wolfish grin before he kissed her and then there was no more talking for a long while.

* * * * *